J 328.45
V235h

DETROIT PUBLIC LIBRARY

P9-EFJ-231

CHASE BRANCH LIBRARY
17731 W. SEVEN MILE RD.
DETROIT, MI 48235

DEC 10

CH

HOW TO BE A
ZOMBIE

SERENA VALENTINO

HOW TO BE A

ZOMBIE

The Essential Guide for Anyone Who Craves Brains

CANDLEWICK PRESS

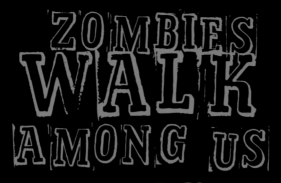

ZOMBIES WALK AMONG US

Have you noticed your thinking process slowing down a bit? Maybe you're craving human flesh like never before, and your scent is getting a little ripe? Have you considered that you may be becoming a member of the undead? Don't worry! While the hype would have you believe that being a zombie is all rotting and eating brains, that's just not true. In fact, zombification is just the first step in a superfun and exciting adventure.

How does a mere mortal such as myself know? Glad you asked. I've always had a soft spot in my heart for zombies but had only admired them from afar. That all changed when a young zombie moved into my apartment building. I noticed this poor fellow had trouble with many things humans take for granted: getting dressed properly, making friends, entertaining at home, and eating a nutritious diet. He often seemed sad because humans were mean to him. I decided I had to help.

I did a little research, interviewed some leading members of the zombie community, and put together a little tip sheet to help him get through everyday life in style and with pride. Over time I watched while he blossomed as a zombie. And I was gratified when he thought to share my helpful tips with his zombie pals. That little list of handy hints grew into the book you hold in your hands today.

Read on and learn how much fun you can have as a zombie. After all, with more and more zombies made every day, you may just end up as one—whether you'd planned to or not. Wouldn't you like to know how to best enjoy your new life as a member of the nonliving?

Serena Valentino

CONTENTS

Fearsome Fashion and Frightful Fun

Adventures in Advanced Zombiedom

Enrich Your Brains

HOW TO JOIN
THE HIDEOUS LEGION OF THE UNDEAD

If you are determined to learn the secrets of zombies, then read on to encounter a shocking spectacle of **epic proportions!** You will find **romance** (in all its vexing forms), bloodcurdling screams, **mind-altering** discoveries (such as what to expect once you have become a **brain-eating** member of the Legion of the Undead), the best ways to find those tasty brain meats, how becoming a zombie actually happens, the various sorts of zombies you will encounter while **walking among the undead** . . . and so much more, all presented especially for you in **spooktacular,** never-before-seen **zombievision!** You will be **paralyzed with fear,** tingling with excitement, and **shocked beyond imagination** at the startling information you will discover in this chapter of *How to Be a Zombie!*

WHAT IS YOUR ZOMBIE ARCHETYPE?

Since brain activity isn't one of your strong points, you may not know what type of zombie you are. This helpful quiz should clear up those nagging questions and allow you to find your place in the world of the undead. So grab a pencil with your rotting hand and enjoy!

1

Where do you feel most at home?

A. Someplace isolated, where I can scream insults and incantations at any luckless mortals I encounter.
B. Post-apocalyptic urban spaces are best, but anywhere I can kill people is fine.
C. Partying it up in a graveyard.
D. Acting cool at the poshest club.

2

When faced with a human pointing a shotgun at you, how do you react?

A. Summon a scream from the pits of hell, terrifying the human into submission.
B. Attack before he gets a chance to load the ammo.

C. Just be my charming, friendly self. I'm sure he'll want to hang out and put down the gun.
D. Shamble away. A bullet might ruin my new limited-edition T-shirt!

3

How do you feel about humans?

A. They must all be destroyed and sent to eternal torment!
B. Must eat them. Kill. Kill. Kill.
C. They're fun to hang out with, but I will snack on them if I get a bout of the munchies.
D. They are *so* last millennium.

4 What's your dream vacation?

A. Returning to the hideous realm from whence I sprang.
B. *Raaaarrgh!* Eating humans is the only thing that matters.
C. Every day is a bloody vacation.
D. Does going on vacation mean leaving the mall? If so, I'll pass.

5 How did you become a zombie?

A. I was summoned by unholy incantations from a forbidden book.
B. Someone vomited blood on me and now I eat everyone in sight.
C. I was in the graveyard with my friends when some creepy old dudes with no skin bit us.
D. What? Isn't the designer sunglasses store around here?

6 What type of outfit do you prefer to wear?

A. I am clad in the rotting flesh in which my unholy master placed me.
B. Can't tell. I'm covered in blood.
C. Band shirt, tight black pants, studded belt, leather jacket, boots.
D. Something hip that my friends will like and comment on.

If your answers are:

Mostly A's You are a necromantic zombie, servant of the dark lords. More than likely, you're a lower demon summoned to Earth by incantation to inhabit the dead, reanimating their flesh. You delight in tormenting the living in unusually cruel ways and driving them to the brink of insanity and death.

Mostly B's You are a rage-virus zombie. You are fueled by livid insanity and the insatiable need to devour as many humans as possible. You are strong, fast, and incredibly deadly, but your mental powers are virtually nil.

Mostly C's You're a party zombie. You enjoy hanging out with friends and having a good time. You're sensible, witty (for your kind), well dressed, and most likely to have friends among humans.

Mostly D's You are a zombster. You spend your time hanging out in shopping malls with your like-minded friends. You travel in packs and consume whatever you want, be it brains or the newest fashions.

KNOW YOUR ZOMBIES

Tales of the walking dead pervade every culture. The first stories of reanimated corpses, rooted in voodoo belief, haunt the folklore of the Caribbean and plantation-era Louisiana. But it's only within the last half-century that the full flowering of zombie culture has occurred. From ghouls with bad attitudes to victims of mysterious viruses, there's a zombie type to fit every end-of-the-world scenario. Here are a few to look for.

CLASSIC

Classic Zombie

The classic zombie is slow, shambling, and dim-witted. What it lacks in speed it makes up for in its ability to frighten: human survivors often lose their senses in its presence and shoot one another.

Cause of transformation Mysterious plague or a bite from another zombie.

Habitat Rural Pennsylvania.

Weaknesses Shotguns and incineration.

Tip Will eat all human flesh, not just the brains.

Brain activity 🧠

Rage-Virus Zombie

This relatively new breed of zombie is fast, deadly, and highly contagious. A human's chance of surviving an encounter with a rage-virus zombie is minimal but not unheard of.

Cause of transformation Blood contamination or zombie bite.

Habitats Great Britain; the whole world (if given the chance).

Weaknesses Gunfire or use of other weaponry on the head.

Tip Will vomit blood, causing humans to contract the virus.

Brain activity 🧠 🧠

RAGE

Necromantic Zombie

Gruesome, terrifying, and vile, these zombies are actually spirits from another realm summoned to inhabit necrotic (that is, dead) flesh.

Cause of transformation Beckoned from a terrifying and inconceivable darkness into a dead human's body.

Habitat Rural New England.

Weakness Can be banished with ancient incantations.

Tip *The Book of the Dead*—an ancient and evil text—is a good resource for both conjuring and banishing these spirits.

Brain activity 🧠 🧠 🧠

NECROMANTIC

ZOMBSTER

Zombster

These hipster zombies make the rounds in groups, wearing fashionable clothes, large sunglasses, and—if they're male—some sort of facial hair. More concerned with their outfits than their appetites, zombsters aren't big on confrontation and don't eat as many brains as other zombies do.

Cause of transformation Virus.

Habitat Large cities.

Weakness Blow to the head.

Tip Easily distracted by shiny objects.

Brain activity

Party Zombie

These music-loving members of the undead are resourceful, love to party in graveyards, and keep half dogs as pets. Humans may find them fun to hang out with, though these zombies are quite honest about wanting to devour human brains!

Cause of transformation Poison gas or contaminated rain; bites from other zombies.

Habitats Cemeteries, crematoriums, and churchyards.

Weakness Burning.

Tip Can survive without their heads.

Brain activity

PARTY

VOODOO

Voodoo Zombie

Buried alive and dug up later by the powerful sorcerers who created them, these tragic creatures have lost their identity and will. While they don't eat brains, they may hunt humans for even more disturbing items: their lives, memories, and souls.

Cause of transformation Magic, along with a potent dose of zombie powder.

Habitat Haiti.

Weakness Some may be restored to life by salt.

Tip Docile and suggestible.

Brain activity 🧠 🧠

PIRATE

Pirate Zombie

Treasure hunters fear encounters with these adventurous and highly fashionable zombies. Pirate zombies seek treasure, not brains, and are usually zombified with a curse rather than via contamination. Just don't get between them and their gold pieces, or you may find yourself at the business end of a sword.

Cause of transformation Curse.

Habitats Pirate ships, seaports, gallows, and damp caves.

Weakness Enchanted treasure.

Tip Usually appear as zombies only after dark.

Brain activity

PET

Pet Zombie

Reanimated rabbits, cats, dogs, and crows are just as vicious as their undead owners, if not worse. Hardwired for instinct and self-preservation, these creatures make fine zombie companions.

Cause of transformation Methods range from burial in cursed cemeteries to eating contaminated flesh.

Habitat Everywhere.

Weakness Destroying their brains will finish off these ghastly creatures.

Tip Deadly to unarmed humans.

Brain activity 🧠

White-Collar Zombie

These undead prowl office buildings, seeking tasty cubicle dwellers. Many report that being a zombie isn't too different from typing or filing. Indeed, many don't regret their fate: they're glad they got zombified before the stock market crashed and they had to pay off their mortgages in the burbs.

Cause of transformation Fast-acting virus or contact with other zombies.

Habitats Corporate buildings, banks, and office-supply stores.

Weaknesses A firm blow to the head; a layoff.

Tip They're not unreasonable—they promise not to eat your eyes.

Brain activity 🧠 🧠 🧠

WHITE-COLLAR

HOW ZOMBIFICATION HAPPENS

There are many ways one can become a zombie. While infection with a deadly plague is most traditional, the zombie apocalypse may come in a number of ways. Remember, no matter how you were zombified, you can always infect others with a simple bite or maybe even by spewing blood on them. No need to go looking for more poison gas or a stray comet!

Viral Infection

This is one of the most common methods of reanimation. There are various strains of the zombie virus, notably "traditional" plague and the newfangled rage virus, which makes for lethal, fast-running zombies.

Poison Gas

If you want to be zombified, keep an eye out for crusty old barrels of mysterious fluid, especially those that bear insignia from any sort of military organization.

Cursed Earth

In Italy, there's a little graveyard that's famous for reanimating the nicest corpses. And in a sleepy Maine town, there's a pet cemetery with equally zombilicious powers.

Space Invaders

When the Earth passes through a comet's tail, crazy things can happen. If the comet is particularly deadly, anyone who stays up late to watch it streak across the sky will turn into a zombie. Other reported cases have been caused by the exposure of hapless humans to toxic radiation from outer space.

Possession by Evil Spirits

In a realm beyond mortal experience lies a mysterious book known as the *Necronomicon*, a tome invented by H. P. Lovecraft and rumored to be full of incantations that allow sorcerers to reanimate the dead with vengeful spirits.

Pure Evil

Some humans were so vile in life that their evil pursues them in death. This despicable force reanimates their dead flesh so that they may continue their wicked, destructive ways.

Voodoo

A *bokor*, or traditional voodoo sorcerer, has the power to transform living people into the walking dead using a powerful brain-numbing potion.

Mad Scientists

These brilliant but unbalanced members of the scientific community can create depraved serums for bringing life to dead flesh, although they often destroy themselves in the process. Zombies made in this fashion, much like those created by voodoo curses, are usually at the whim of their "masters."

Becoming a member of the undead transports you into a dangerous and beautiful world filled with terror, hideous allure, and exploration. You are venturing into a dark and treacherous realm. Embrace your newfound freedoms with the dignity and resolve they require.

> Scene from *28 Days Later* (2002)

ANATOMY OF A ZOMBIE

Becoming a zombie is an interesting and frightening experience. Depending on your particular type, the exact nature of the transformation will vary. Sometimes the change is instantaneous; in other cases, your transition into an undead creature may take hours or even weeks. In general, most zombies can expect to pass through the following symptoms, stages, and changes. Remember, as with so many things in life, it may be tough, but the result is so worth it!

Disorientation and Nausea

Your body is changing . . . fast! Soon, you'll be a fully fledged member of the army of the dead, but right now your immune system just thinks you have a really bad flu. Lie down for a bit, but be sure to do it somewhere nice and safe. No need to freak out the school nurse!

Rigor Mortis

Pretty quickly (usually within two to four hours after contamination), your muscles will start to stiffen up. You'll probably feel it first in your jaw. Ask a friendly human to help you stretch, and, once your transformation is complete, consider taking up yoga to stay limber.

Changing Senses

You'll suddenly be able to see, hear, and smell things you never detected when you were alive—even if your eyes eventually fall out and your nose rots off. Plus, you'll be able to see in the dark, making hunting so much easier.

Speech Impediment

Very few zombies retain the power of speech. You may notice yourself groaning, wheezing, and making other weird noises. If you're a necromantic zombie, you'll probably start cursing humans and making fancy-sounding threats.

Getting Around

In most cases, zombification makes you calmer and slower moving. If you've gotten the rage virus (or one of a few other infection types), you may instead find yourself hopped up and running around like crazy. Either way, just have fun! Whether you're chilling on the couch or hastening the apocalypse, it's all good.

The Long Haul

Some zombie experts claim that all zombies eventually stop functioning. This is an urban legend. With proper care, any zombie can have a long, fulfilling reanimation. Supplement brains with leafy greens and take your vitamins.

Lungs

Most of the undead keep breathing out of habit (and so they can make those gnarly groaning noises). However, you actually don't need oxygen anymore. Try taking a walk underwater! The fish will never know what bit them.

Brain

It'll be . . . different. Not so many worrying thoughts, just peaceful silence and the unending hunger for flesh. Some zombies retain a surprising amount of brain function, and studies show that staying active and social can help.

Jaw

It's not unusual for a zombie's jaw to get stuck in the open position. No worries; you will quite literally feel no discomfort, and it makes eating (and spewing blood on your victims) much easier!

Spinal Column

The spine's nerves allow humans to feel pain. Good news—all that's over for you! You will never feel pain again, unless you're one of those zombies who eats to stave off the pain of decomposition. (Okay, you'll never feel much of anything again, but still, it's pretty cool.)

Adrenal Glands

Many zombies are kind of sluggish, but those infected with the rage virus have a constant stream of adrenaline rushing through their bodies, urging them to create havoc.

Digestion

Your organs may barely be there, but boy, can you eat! Scientists haven't quite figured out how zombies can eat so much flesh— even when their entrails are sticking out of their bodies— but luckily for you, it doesn't seem to pose a problem. Eat hearty!

ZOMBIE DAY PLANNER

SUNDAY

- 9:30 AM: Dr. Herbert West to discuss his recent medical experiments
- GO GROCERY SHOPPING

MONDAY

- CANCEL GYM MEMBERSHIP
- Embalming fluid—available online?
- PET SUPPLY STORE—STURDY METAL CAGE FOR DORIAN

TUESDAY

- HUNTING—RESTOCK THE BASEMENT WITH HUMANS
- 8 PM: friends over for dinner
- 10:30 PM: KARAOKE

WEDNESDAY

- steam-clean the carpet
- CHECK OUT SHOPPING MALL WITH THE GANG

AUGUST

THURSDAY
- 1 AM: FUNERAL HOME FOR MAKEUP APPOINTMENT
- 11 PM: party in the cemetery
- PRANK CALLS TO LOCAL POLICE STATION

FRIDAY
- 10 AM: meet with insurance agent (don't eat him!!!).
Can I collect on my life insurance?
- BUY PLASTIC WRAP / 8:30 PM: DATE WITH SHAUN

SATURDAY
- PET SUPPLY STORE—RAT BRAINS FOR DORIAN
- Call shaun—did I leave my arm in his car last night?

AUGUST

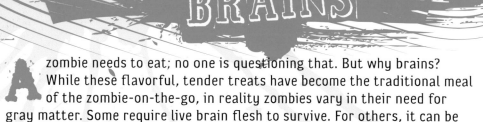

TASTY HUMAN BRAINS

A zombie needs to eat; no one is questioning that. But why brains? While these flavorful, tender treats have become the traditional meal of the zombie-on-the-go, in reality zombies vary in their need for gray matter. Some require live brain flesh to survive. For others, it can be an occasional snack or delicacy. Let your own body be your guide.

Feeding the Need

Zombies eat brains for a variety of reasons. Brains are tasty and also high in protein and nutrients. They are soft and easy on the gums (which is helpful for zombies who have lost teeth). For many zombies, especially those created by poison gas, brains are actually a basic necessity: being deprived of them for any period of time causes great suffering, and the only treatment is to hunt and eat until the pain subsides.

When Brains Are Brain Food

Some zombies believe that a brain-rich diet helps their mental function. The homeopathic theory that "like treats like" supports this idea. In other words, to improve a brain, eat a brain! Others go further than this, preferring different types of brains for different occasions or needs.

Meals on the Go

While some zombies have been known to keep live humans around for their snacking pleasure, others find this a bit labor-intensive. An alternative is breaking into mortuaries, scientific-research laboratories, morgues, or other locations where dead bodies are located. Rely on these places for a quick and easy snack (much like a fast-food drive-through), or fill your zombie-mobile with treats for later. Zombie metabolism can be quirky, so experiment with these convenience foods to make sure that they agree with you and that you're getting the needed nutrients.

A Zombie's Foremost Rule

Whatever your reason for eating brains (or other flesh, for that matter), rest assured that there will always be plenty for you to devour as long as you follow this simple rule: finish everything. If any brain remains, your victim will become a zombie who competes with you for a dwindling supply of human flesh. Plus, it will make your mother happy to see you clean your plate.

The Humanitarian Zombie

Interestingly enough, a small number of zombies don't eat humans at all. Instead, they prefer animal brains, usually served raw. Some have ranches where they raise cattle, goats, and pigs. An entrepreneurial few have taken it even further, packaging their products and selling them to other like-minded zombies for a tidy profit.

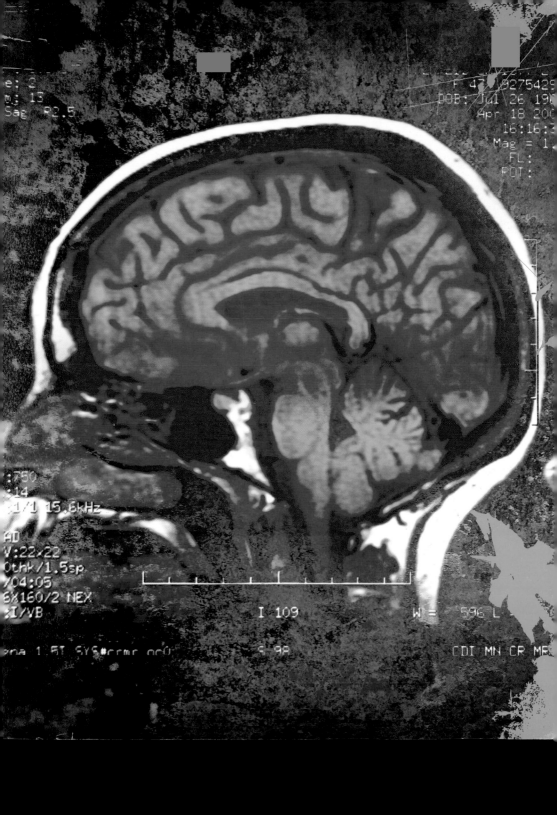

THE HUNT IS ON!

Humans—they can be enemies, friends, even loved ones. But most of all, they're food. If you're not lucky enough to live near a zombie farmers' market where you can pick up ready-to-eat brain meats, you'll have to hunt your own. These hints can help improve your diet.

Choose Your Meal

Many zombies have noted that different brains not only have unique flavors but may actually transfer some of the victim's traits to the lucky diner. If you're feeling a bit slow, you might want to try munching down a college professor. Ready to get romantic? A poet's brain may help you woo that special someone. As for flavor, nice people are rumored to have sweeter brains. If someone looks friendly, they'll probably taste good. For some reason, rock musicians taste terrible—but if you really want those guitar skills, it might be worth choking one down.

The Tools at Hand

It's pretty easy to just grab a human and start munching. However, if you'd like to add a little more finesse to your dining, consider using specialized tools. For instance, the ancient Egyptians used a long metal hook to remove a person's brains through their nose before making them into a mummy. A large crochet hook should work nicely. If you want to get all fancy-pants, the proper name for this is an *endonasal operation*. If that's too complicated, a jigsaw tool will open that skull right up without damaging the brains.

Find and Feed

In the early days of any zombie virus infestation, humans won't really understand what's happening. Take advantage of this moment to hunt in places where you can find big hordes of them in a pacified state—say, in line to renew their driver's licenses. Later, they become wilier and hole up in bunkers, forts, and maximum-security prisons. To pick off the foolhardy, hunt at night, when you'll be able to see lights in the windows. Careful: any meal that looks too easy to catch may be a trap.

Basic Table Manners

Zombies often hunt in packs, and sometimes feeding can be a free-for-all frenzy. Try to bring a little dignity to the proceedings. Always offer guests the first bite, and never bite and run. There may not be dishes to wash or a table to clear, but it's still considered polite to engage in a little postprandial conversation.

When a Human Isn't Food

Trying to convert your friends into a zombie posse? Bite them just enough to infect them. On the other hand, if you don't want a certain person to reanimate, eat the entire brain.

ALTERNATIVE FOODS

Many zombie old-timers find it shocking that "these new breeds of zombies" (as they call them) don't enjoy the entire banquet of flesh that is available. Other zombies just don't like the taste of brains. Whatever the reason, you can eschew human brains and still eat well.

The Case Against Brains

Brains are outrageously high in cholesterol, and they can cause brain-wasting conditions such as Creutzfeldt-Jakob disease (which is related to mad cow disease) and kuru. Luckily for you, you no longer have to worry about silly little illnesses. But if you share your treats with a human companion, it's a good idea to mix up the menu a bit with non-human-based meals, lest you turn a friend into a cannibal. On your own, you can also try eating other body parts—you might actually like them!

Blood, Guts, and Gore

Traditional slow and slack-jawed zombies tend to eat just about anything living they can get their hands on. The entire human is up for grabs with these zombies (though they do seem to be particularly fond of entrails), and they'll devour as much as they can before another human comes and tries to do them in. Similarly, rage-virus zombies aren't really fussy about what they eat. They'll pretty much tear into any portion of the human. One hint? Don't just take a bite and move on. Many zombies get overexcited by the hunt and forget that a single human can last for several meals. Not so hungry at the moment? Take the leftovers home and freeze them for later.

Haute Cuisine

Some zombies out there believe themselves to be more civilized than their bloodthirsty brethren and tend to eat fancier dishes— many of which aren't made of humans at all. If you're a zombie with discriminating taste, world cuisine has an amazing array of brain-based dishes to offer. An advantage of relishing these delicacies is that they're served in many upscale restaurants, so you can dine with human friends. A sampling of what you may find includes French braised calf's brains, fried brains Roman-style with lemon and bread crumbs, Indonesian cooked brains in coconut cream, hearty German brain soup, Indian roasted goat brain, Cuban brain fritters, Parmesan-crumbed lambs' brains, and scrambled eggs with fresh pork brains.

The "Adventurous" Palate

There are a lot of alternatives to brains—go ahead, experiment! Do you love the squishy texture of brains, but don't have the time to hunt? Maybe macaroni and cheese would be nice. Is it brains' lovely grayish-white color you're craving? Cauliflower and oatmeal both fit the bill. And if you're looking to boost your own brain function, try foods rich in omega-3 fatty acids, like salmon.

WHEN HUMANS ATTACK

Let's face the facts: Once you and your zombie buddies start bringing about the end of civilization as we know it, humans are going to get annoyed. And violent. Here's what you need to know to evade these human pests. Read carefully, and stay safe out there!

Who Hunts Zombies?

When you think of zombie hunters, you may imagine a lone human out there in the woods, shovel in hand, ready to take you on *mano a mano.* In truth, the human threat takes many forms. Individual vigilantes are indeed a problem. More worrisome, however, are organized groups and government-sponsored SWAT teams. People take the end of the world really seriously for some reason, and whole armies may be mobilized against you. How can you survive this? A few handy hints can make a big difference.

Keep Your Head

It's hard to keep your wits about you when you're a zombie, but the most important thing you need to remember is to stay aware. Use your superior senses of sight, smell, and hearing to be on the alert for humans. If you hear a whole bunch of them together, think "Danger!" instead of "Buffet!" Never tell your human friends where you live until you really, really trust them. And finally, beware of humans dressed like zombies. They may be trying to infiltrate and attack. Some even go so far as to rub zombie flesh all over themselves to mask their delicious odor.

Know Your Surroundings

Many zombies enjoy hunting in the backwoods. Unfortunately, the people who live in these spots are often armed and don't take kindly to "freaks of nature" in their territory. In urban areas, neighborhood-watch communities have reorganized as zombie patrols. Look for telltale signposts featuring a watchful eye with the letter *Z* superimposed.

Fight for Your Rights

Humans don't fight fair. They may come at you with flamethrowers, shotguns, even nuclear warheads. It's hard to defend against this stuff—just lie low until they leave. When humans are foolish enough to try hand-to-hand combat, however, you're golden. Don't get caught up in the thrill of battle—just bite them and be done with it so you can move on to the next assailant. If they're wielding pickaxes, shovels, or other improvised tools, dodge to direct the blows away from your head to less essential parts of your anatomy. (Your brain is the only part you need to protect.) Savvy zombies have taken to wearing helmets and light body armor when they go out. You can find a great selection at sporting-goods stores or motorcycle shops.

UNDEAD FOES

Sad to say, zombies are pretty low on the undead food chain. Faster, smarter, and more powerful entities may try to take advantage of you. Here are some unfriendlies to avoid.

Werewolves

When you're out hunting humans, especially in wooded rural areas, keep a sharp eye out for werewolves. Depending on the type of werewolf you encounter (that is, whether its transformation is lunar- or emotion-triggered), you could be unexpectedly attacked. Above all, you don't want to surprise one, provoking it into transforming. Werewolves are strong enough to rip the average zombie's head clean off its shoulders in the blink of an eye. So make some inquiries just to be safe. Any werewolves in the area? Where do they hang out? And maybe stock up on edibles before the full moon if you have any concerns. Sometimes it's just safer to eat leftovers rather than go out.

Vampires

Depending on their clan and its value system, vampires can be quite dangerous to zombies. To be safe, it's best to avoid all vampires, no matter how enticing they may be. Sometimes, a vampire will pretend to be your friend for the purpose of luring you to one of his special parties. Once you're there, he may try to enslave you and use you for entertainment, forcing you to fight other members of the undead gladiator-style. If you live in an area populated by vampires, take the same precautions humans do to keep yourself safe

Mummies

Out of the entire undead population, mummies are by far the most aristocratic. Simply because they're of royal descent and went through life believing they were the living representatives of the gods, they are hopeless snobs. Also, they're sensitive about brains, having lost their own through their noses long ago. Mummies will kill zombies on the spot. No discussion, no warning—dead. Zombies are, in the mummy's opinion, an abomination, a violation against the gods. Luckily, most mummies walk about even more slowly than zombies, so you shouldn't have much trouble getting away. And get away you should. You don't want to mess with a mummy.

Witches

Immortal, bone-munching hags like Baba Yaga have been known to enslave zombies to do domestic chores around the hut, feeding them scant morsels of brains as pay. If witches weren't so wickedly cruel, this could be a good arrangement, but there's no free lunch! Witches will work you hard, refuse to give you any time off, and place mean spells on you just for fun. If one of them approaches you, shamble away from her as fast as you can. And whatever you do, do not enter her hut, even if she is dangling gray matter like a succulent little treat before your eyes!

VAMPIRE: SCARY PARTIES. STAY HOME INSTEAD.

WEREWOLF: BIG TEETH. DON'T LET HIM BITE.

MUMMY: MOVES SLOW BUT NOT NICE. RUN AWAY!

WITCH: SHE'S A BAD BOSS. DON'T EAT THOSE BRAINS!

ROAM ALONE OR IN PACKS?

The choice between roaming alone or traveling in packs all depends on the lifestyle you want to lead. Whether you were a party animal or a loner in life, you'll probably be the same when you're a zombie.

Traveling in Packs

Do you want to cause havoc with your fellow members of the undead, stirring up trouble as you move from town to town and city to city, bringing death and infection to all you encounter? If so, a zombie pack is right for you. Being in a group can give you a huge adrenaline rush, not to mention feelings of zombie pride and solidarity. Many zombies report that brain hunting *en masse* is more thrilling and satisfying than hunting alone. And wouldn't you rather be with your zombie friends if you run into some humans?

Your Very Own Outbreak

So you want to become a zombie but really don't want to give up all of your awesome friends. Don't worry; you can have it all—just start your own zombie infestation! It's very important to make sure that anyone you convert really wants to be a zombie—it's not the sort of thing you do to someone as a birthday surprise or practical joke. But if a bunch of you really get along well, why not? Zombie hordes have been started by football teams, Girl Scout troops, and at least one middle-school chess team. Other zombies may call you a snobby clique, but so what? They're just jealous.

The Downside of Pack Life

A huge mass of brain-crazed zombies is a beautiful sight to behold—but it does tend to get the humans worked up. Everything from pointy sticks to nuclear bombs can and will be used against you when humans feel threatened. If you'd rather not go around feeling like there's a huge target painted on your head, then you might be happier solo.

Roam Alone

Some zombies find it's possible to settle down somewhere and live a "normal" life. This choice is a good one if you've still got some memories, not to mention higher brain function. Being by yourself gives you the chance to hunt discreetly, which can help reduce your stress. It's an individual choice, and some zombies have made it work.

The Importance of Staying Social

Choosing not to join a pack doesn't mean you can't hang out with other zombies. In fact, you should. It's important to be with others who understand you and share your interests. If you like, you can find a middle ground by going to concerts, parties, and parades with others of your kind, while still hunting and hunkering down alone.

LIVING WITH HUMANS

Some zombies see humans simply as food or prey, while others like to socialize with understanding human companions. For their part, certain humans enjoy the low-key, chill attitude zombies bring to everything (except hunting). And then there are those humans who just want to be part of whatever's in, even if it's a highly contagious virus.

Some Humans Love Zombies

You won't have to worry about expensive and bothersome "beauty" appointments with these humans. They love you as you are—wounds, missing limbs, and all. Certain "zombie groupies" can get quite annoying with their overenthusiastic curiosity, but most of the time they mean well and should not be snacked on. You might try to gently redirect their interest in how different you are into helping you seem *less* different to the rest of the world. Your mortal friends can give you tips on how to adjust your clothing, attitude, and habits to better blend in.

Hunting with Humans

Regardless of how open-minded and curious your human friends may be, it's not a good idea to take them hunting. No matter how many horror movies they've seen, the reality is going to freak them out. Some of them may be willing to lure unsuspecting victims back to your home, which can be very helpful. Don't rely on them for all your meals, though—you want to keep your hunting skills sharp.

Making Human Friends

Sometimes it seems like everyone's against the poor, hapless zombie. What with those SWAT teams, army officers, vigilantes, and overeducated college nerds trying to take you down, it's easy to forget to just reach out and make a connection. In looking for kindred souls, seek out open-minded, quirky types. Goths, punks, art students, and gamers are often friendly to zombies. In addition, undertakers, prostheticians, and sci-fi writers on the whole tend to have a rather morbid sense of humor, which makes them more likely to "get" you.

Be a Good Friend

Humans may be willing to score you fake limbs, help you dress well, and feed you. It's important that you be a good friend in return. Think of the things they may not enjoy that are easy for you. For instance, zombies often do ironing and other household chores because they can't get bored. And if your human friend just likes to sit on the couch and watch TV, you're the perfect companion.

> Scene from *Undead* (2003)

TELLING THE FAMILY

Your friends and family knowing the truth about your transformation might cause you some understandable anxiety. After all, they perhaps won't take too kindly to your new, rather pungent aroma and shocking cravings. You can't really blame them—they may be justifiably frightened in your company and fearful that you will eat their brains.

Assess Your Willpower

First things first: if you care for your friends and family, and it would distress them to undergo zombification, then take a good look at yourself. Do you have what it takes to spend time with your loved ones and resist taking a bite out of them? If so, then by all means, share your news in person.

Put Your Best Face Forward

Take a moment to prepare for this talk. Be sure to dress nicely (blood splatters can really set the wrong tone), and try not to lurch or moan too much. If you're one of the many zombies who have lost their powers of speech, bring a notebook or even a whiteboard. More tech-savvy zombies may prepare a simple slide show presentation that explains their new state of being.

Address Their Anxieties

Your family loves you, and they worry. Assure them that things today are a lot different than they were back in the old days. Today, many zombies hold down jobs, have human friends, and really enjoy their postmortem experience. If your parents feel the need for support,

direct them to one of the zombie friends-and-family support groups that are springing up in cities and towns across the globe.

Be Prepared for Anything

In some cases, no matter how delicately you approach the situation, your family and friends may become unreasonably frightened and behave irrationally, maybe calling the police or grabbing torches and pitchforks. The next time you come to visit, you might find they have boarded up the windows. Give them time. More likely than not, they'll come around. If you suspect that your family will take the news really badly, start with a phone call or e-mail to test the waters.

Taking the Next Step

After your little talk, be sure to stay for dinner and spend some quality time. Sure, Mom's cooking isn't as tasty as fresh human flesh, but make the sacrifice. Reassure your friends and family that they are not in danger of being contaminated with the zombie virus. If they reply that they'd like to join you, help them understand zombification, including all the (literally) gory details. But not over meatloaf. Make a date to talk at a later time.

< Scene from *Blood of the Zombie: The Dead One* (1961)

HOW TO PASS AS A HUMAN

Zombie pride is an important issue, and activists who stress that you should embrace your condition are absolutely right. Still, there are times when you want to look human. Maybe you're a zombie who needs to work a job and pay rent. Maybe you're dating a squeamish human. Whatever the reason, here are some tips on passing.

Mortician Beauticians

With zombification on the rise, many morticians have taken to moonlighting as restorative artists to the undead. Experienced with making the dead seemly for public presentation, your local mortician can help you with your mortal-mimicking needs. Go to them for everything from filling in those nasty wounds with putty to giving you a nice human-looking skin tone with airbrushing and makeup. And if you happen to have part of your face missing, or an eye that's fallen out, a mortician can help with that, too.

DIY Beauty for the Undead

If you're not a zombie of means, you may not be able to afford professional help. Fret not, there are ways of doing it yourself. Humans use special-effects makeup to look like zombies—why not use the same tricks to make yourself look human? All you need is some liquid latex and cosmetics that match your desired skin tone. Fill in gashes and tears with the latex, allow it to dry, and apply a liquid makeup base. Make sure to set it with pressed powder in a matching shade.

Overcoming Zombie Odor

If you're trying to pass as a human, you really don't want to smell like rotting flesh. Embalming fluid can arrest your putrefaction, or, as a cheap alternative, cologne might work. Use a light hand, because many people would rather smell putrid flesh than too much body spray.

Accessorize for Success

Replacing missing limbs is no big deal if you have access to prosthetics—but don't stop there! A glass eye can really add a human touch to that empty socket. And if some pesky human got you with a flamethrower, a wig may be in order. Finally, if your teeth have been knocked out, dentures are a good idea.

Acting the Part

Humans rarely lurch, moan, or bite each other, so you should cut back on these habits. Work on your posture and gait (a dance class or Pilates session might help), and try not to mumble. If you've lost the power of speech, carry a notebook with you, or communicate by text message. You'll blend right in.

TIPS FOR YOUR HUMAN SWEETIE

Zombies need love too, and mortals may wish to cozy up to one of the zombified—either while deciding whether to join the growing ranks of the undead or just to cuddle with someone who loves them for their brains. But how do you woo mortals safely, with minimal shouting and shovel-wielding? Share this tip sheet with your human crush, and you could soon be shambling off into the sunset with a real live human date!

Contain Leakage

All humans should take a page out of their great-aunt's book and put plastic on the furniture. Although not exactly the height of modern décor, it will keep those nasty spills off your couch should your zombie love start to ooze. A wet vac will come in handy for any carpet-related spills, and keep plastic and duct tape nearby to protect car seats, movie theater seats, and restaurant chairs.

Forgive Mental Lapses

Sometimes your undead sweetheart might be a little slow-witted, so be patient if he forgets important dates from time to time or if he is easily distracted, especially by other girls—more than likely he's thinking about her brains and not her body!

Offer Snacks

It's helpful to make friends with someone in the medical or funerary industry—this way, you'll always have a fresh supply of brains when entertaining the undead. But some zombies can only sustain themselves on live brain tissue. In these situations, better remind your dearest to eat before she comes by.

Use Protection

Depending on the sort of zombie you're dating, it might be a good idea to wear a helmet, just in case he's tempted to take a bite of your sweet brain meats. He does love you, after all, and might not be able to resist a little taste.

Don't Rush into Things

Considering the plastic, duct tape, and weapons needed to safely date a zombie, you might be tempted to forgo the hassle of staying alive and become a zombie yourself. It might make the relationship easier, but you should read this manual completely before deciding to become a brain-eating member of the Legion of the Undead.

Wear Appropriate Clothing

Of course you want to look your best while on a date, but you never know when your darling might grab a nearby waiter and start chomping. As a general rule, humans shou!dn't wear anything they wouldn't want sprayed with blood. It's best to choose clothing made from easily cleaned materials like PVC, latex, and patent leather.

> Scene from *Fido* (2006)

FEARSOME FASHION AND FRIGHTFUL FUN

Hello, brave young zombies. If you've made it this far, you are indeed walking the tombstone-lined path of the undead; you have left the cemetery and are venturing into the perilous mortal world. Though dangerous, this world is full of pleasures, too. This chapter will reveal brain-tingling discoveries, such as outrageously spookarific fashion and makeup advice, as well as the ultimate zombie music playlists, advice on how to turn your precious pets into members of the undead, and so much more! So, my dear devourers of delicious gray matter, go forth and conquer!

ZOMBIE FASHION

It's a common misconception that zombies don't care about their appearance, perhaps because of all those style-impaired movie zombies. In fact, if a human likes to dress well in life, then he or she will want to do the same once undead. Zombies don't tend to rethink the style they dug while alive. Just as there is no one way to dress as a human, there is no single zombie fashion. However, every member of the undead should follow some basic pointers. The most basic? Just because you're dead doesn't mean your sense of style is dead—you can change with the times. Hey, if you don't, you may end up wearing that outfit for a long, long time.

Zombie Fashion Issues

One major issue to consider is that all the hardwiring in a zombie's brain remains intact after the moment of reanimation, but there's usually little room for change or evolution. So, it simply doesn't occur to many zombies that they should change out of the outfits they were killed or buried in. Like those mortals who never stop wearing the clothes that were in style when they were teens, these zombies just don't get that they need to update their look every so often.

Mortal Eye for the Zombie Guy

It's wise to hook up with human friends who can take you to the mall (if you're not there already) and help you choose flattering, durable, easy-to-care-for clothing. Just remember to check labels! Dry-clean–only items are a real hassle when you regularly end up splattered with blood and brain matter. If you really hanker for a fabulous look, you might want to try eating a model or fashion designer in an effort to absorb a sense of style from his or her brains.

Dress for Hunting Success

It's important to be comfortable in whatever you wear. Since zombies no longer have any working nerves, this is not so much about wearing comfy shoes or pants that fit. Rather, it's about being sure you can track down enough prey. If you're one of those trendy new fast-moving zombies, that may not be such a big deal. If, however, you're an old-school, stagger-about type, make sure your clothes aren't too baggy (stopping to pull up your jeans can allow your prey to get away). High heels are a major survival "don't."

Find Your Personal Style

Whether you go for traditional ragged clothing and tasteful blood spatters, a retro and shredded prom dress, or maybe a flamboyant pirate costume, what's important is that the outfit works for you. Ideally, your clothes are a reflection of your inner zombie. In the following pages, we'll look at some popular styles that the undead have sported over the years, as well as some cool and bleeding-edge alternatives.

There is something quite charming about a zombie lad donning a slightly tatty but nevertheless dandy suit.

It conjures images of our beloved and innocent silent-film stars and throws humans off their game.

Blood splatters are always in fashion in zombieworld. They're a prerequisite, actually!

You don't want your brain-eating friends to think you're a poser, do you? So don't be afraid to get a little messy at mealtime.

Sturdy boots are most certainly in order when you're walking among the undead ... and when you're running away from humans with shotguns, too.

PUT YOUR BEST
(MOST HORRIFIC)
FACE FORWARD

For humans who want to test the waters before deciding to become a zombie—or for anyone invited to an undead party—here are some helpful tips for looking like a zombie even when you're still alive.

Getting Your Ghoul On

Decide first of all whether your zombie will be sporting wounds. If so, you'll need to begin with these. You can start with some nice facial wounds using the technique described below. After you've made your wound, follow the tutorial at right to apply your allover makeup. Then finish off with some special effects, like maybe an exposed bone or rotting flesh (see the following pages). Of course, in a pinch, you can skip the fancy effects and just ladle on the gore. But really, a little extra effort will help you blend in so much better.

What You Will Need

Stock your zombification kit with a wide array of cream-based makeup, including green, gray, black, white, blue, brown, purple, and red. You should also have tissue paper or toilet paper (single-ply is best); a fair amount of liquid latex (the makeup that special-effects artists use to create fake skin); and lots of applicators, like craft sticks and makeup sponges. You'll find most of these items at costume or theatrical stores. You can also buy all-in-one kits with most of these ingredients, but choosing your own is more fun.

Make a Hideous Wound

1. Apply a thin layer of latex on the areas of your face where you'd like to create wounds.

2. While the liquid latex is wet, place a few bits of tissue or toilet paper over it.

3. Once the tissue is dry, apply another layer of latex, then carefully tear sections.

Zombify Your Face

Once you've got some nice wounds, you'll want to apply your disgusting, putrid skin color and, of course, buckets of fake blood. Depending on the look you're going for, you might want to vary your palette. Don't be afraid to mix and match colors for various bruise-and-rot combinations. This makeup washes off easily, so unlike with real zombification, do-overs are no problem.

1. Start with a putrid base color—white, green, or gray.

2. Use a darker purple to shade your face's contours.

3. Stipple on your rot in green, yellow, brown, and purple.

4. Line your eyes with dark red for a demonic look.

5. Purplish black is a good look for undead lips.

6. Add black and purple around your liquid latex wounds, plus red for blood.

7. Add more fake blood! You can never have enough blood.

8. Dip a brush or comb in fake blood and scrape it over your skin for scratches.

9. Don't forget hair gel for that killer look.

ADD A LITTLE UNDEAD FLAIR

Look at you! You're beautiful! Now it's time to add some undeadtastic touches, with a few extra tricks of the trade. These advanced tips will take your zombie look to a whole new level of ghastly gorgeousness—plus, they're easy and cheap to achieve. Once you've mastered these faux afflictions, look to your favorite zombie films for new injuries and wounds that you could easily replicate using everyday items.

Show Your Skull

Want to look as if you've narrowly avoided decapitation? An exposed skull can be built up over your makeup base—just wipe the edges clean so that the liquid latex can get a better grip.

1. Cut out a nice swatch of "skull" from a plastic lid.

2. Clean the spot you'd like to "expose," then place the plastic lid over a thick patch of liquid latex.

3. Layer over the edges of the plastic lid with more liquid latex to make it look less tacked on. When the liquid dries, add makeup and, of course, red for blood.

Sprinkle on Maggots

You might think that the food chain ends with zombies eating brains, but maggots will feed on pretty much anything, including rotting flesh. So if you want to look especially gruesome by faking an infestation of creepy-crawlies, here's how you do it!

1. Lay down some liquid latex.

2. While the liquid latex is still moist, sprinkle on a few pinches of white rice.

3. Build up the edges with more liquid latex. When it dries, add makeup "bruises."

Create an Exposed Bone

No undead look is complete without a broken bone jutting out through the skin! The exposed bone can work on your arm or leg, or, if you're feeling really ambitious, you could make an entire set of splintery ribs—no trip to the emergency room required!

1. Cut a length of "bone" from a white candle.

2. Stick it to your arm (or wherever) with liquid latex.

3. Once it is dry, add some nice bruise texture with makeup and, as always, gobs of fake blood.

SHAMBLE AMONG THE UNDEAD AS A CLASSIC ROMERO ZOMBIE!

A true classic, the George Romero zombie—based on the stellar black-and-white 1968 film *Night of the Living Dead*—assumes the clothing and appearance of 1960s suburbanites and turns them into a thing of horror. This touchstone of zombie culture never grows old, no matter how many decades have passed since it first terrified audiences. So, impress your friends—and perhaps even your parents—by dressing like a classic Romero zombie.

Creepy Color Palette

For a uniquely creepy look, go as a zombie from the original black-and-white movie. (Many of Romero's later zombie flicks were in color.) Choose clothing in shades of black, white, and gray, and do your makeup in the same tones. Dark gray shadows under your eyes and cheekbones are particularly effective. Go with black or red blood—black is really scary-looking, but buckets of bright red on your stark outfit would look pretty cool, too.

Fabulous Fashions

The power of this zombie lies in subverting everyday archetypes (like, say, the girl next door) and making them completely terrifying. Look for clothing that could be from the late 1960s, like polyester suits for men or miniskirts with turtleneck sweaters and go-go boots for ladies. And don't forget to make your outfit look tatty, muddied, and torn—after all, you've just crawled out of the grave.

Arm Yourself with Accessories

People are somewhat mistaken when they think the classic Romero zombie isn't very bright. In the original film, zombie Karen wields a garden trowel to deadly effect. This may have started the trend of more evolved zombies carrying shovels—they're great for fending off zombie hunters, plus you can dig up new friends and infect them!

Basic Behavior

Night of the Living Dead is the movie that brought zombies into the modern era, and many of the media assumptions about how zombies act are based on depictions from this film. Stick together in nice big groups, walk slowly, and don't act too bright. You're frightened of fire, but you consider barbecued human flesh a tasty treat. Unlike modern zombies, you're not so into the brains—you prefer to just grab the nearest human and start chomping.

< Scene from *Dawn of the Dead* (1978)

FRIGHTEN YOUR FOES AS A RAGE-VIRUS ZOMBIE

You totally redefine the zombie mythology, you rebel. Fast, fearsome, and dangerous, the rage-virus zombie is a sight to behold. Known for their manic movements and their fondness for vomiting blood on their victims, these zombies terrify all who encounter them.

The Look: Basic and Bloody

You can wear just about anything you like and be an effective rage-virus zombie. The real key is making sure that you include tons of blood. Rage-virus zombies' skin tones aren't necessarily as ashen as those of other zombies, because the transformation is so quick that there isn't much time for rotting. You could still have some nasty wounds, though—you may not be a reanimated corpse, but you're still likely to be injured fighting humans. Your clothing should be ripped and saturated with blood and gore. What to wear? Well, since the rage infection began in England, give a shout-out to your Brit origins with skinny jeans, black boots, and an Oasis T-shirt or maybe a nice Union Jack design. A Babyshambles T would also be funny.

The Eyes Have It

If it's within your means, a pair of red contact lenses can really bring your look together—eerie red eyes are a hallmark of this zombie. Otherwise, just rim your eyes in scary red eyeliner or stage makeup for a similar effect.

Recipe for Revulsion

You can't have too much blood covering you as a rage-virus zombie. That much fake blood could get pricey, so consider making your own. Mix a cup of thick corn syrup with ten drops of red food coloring and one drop of green. Stir well. If the color isn't gross enough, add a drop of black color. This recipe is totally nontoxic, so you can spew all the blood you want out of your mouth without worry. It's also fun to fill a plastic bag with a few cups of this fake blood, run a plastic tube into it, and tape the whole assembly under your clothes, with the tube sticking out of your shirt's neckhole. Secretly squeeze the bag and blood will "vomit" out near your mouth.

Get Up and Go

Unlike the majority of zombies, you have no problems with coordination. You're fast and furious! Have fun with this unusual zombie power, and do things that ordinary zombies can't. Maybe try dominating at soccer (remember, it's considered bad form to eat the referee) or dancing to the latest tunes.

DEEPLY DISTURB AS A HAUNTING VOODOO ZOMBIE

The voodoo zombie wanders in an ethereal, ghostly manner almost as if lost in a mist, haunting our imaginations and bringing our deepest fears to the surface. These zombies look like blank slates, but they are actually sentient souls trapped within themselves, seeking their identities and clues about their past lives.

The Look: Simple and Unsettling

This can be one of the easier zombie looks to achieve, but it's one of the most tragic and frightening. Men can don a pair of simple trousers with a rope belt and white shirt. For women, a white flowing dress works well. Since you'll be dressed however the sorcerer who made you feels is appropriate, you can go for a classic rural look or something more like a uniform. What if that sorcerer was raising an army to do his will? How would he or she dress you?

Subtle Makeup

Voodoo zombies aren't gruesome-looking like other zombies—they simply look dead in an uncanny way. Make your face pale and gaunt with the application of light face paint or powder. Dark circles around your eyes are key—make them with black or dark-purple eye makeup. Add to your otherworldly eeriness by adorning your forehead with a smudged black cross, or try a disturbing-looking symbol of your own creation.

Dust and Coffin Dirt

Be sure to apply dirt or dust to your face and clothes. Talcum powder works well to give your face and clothing an ashen look. Try mixing the powder with a dark spice like cinnamon or nutmeg from your kitchen cupboard to impart a darker color that looks more like grave dirt. You can, of course, always go outside and get yourself some good old-fashioned dirt as well.

Tools of the Trade

Voodoo zombies are created as slaves to do chores for their masters. You might consider carrying a shovel, rake, or other implement to symbolize this.

Act the Part

It's important to act the part when you dress like a voodoo zombie. You walk slowly, in a dreamlike state. Your eyes should be open wide, with a glazed, lost look as if you're searching for something you may never actually find: your identity and former life!

FIND BEAUTY IN DEATH AS A DAY OF THE DEAD ZOMBIE

In Mexico the dead are invited to an annual celebration on November 2, when they are honored with altars adorned with marigolds, chocolates, sweet breads, and sugar skulls. One can't tell the living from the deceased on the Day of the Dead—el Día de los Muertos—because humans and the dead walk and dance among each other, as it is meant to be on this beautiful candlelit holiday.

The Look: Beautiful and Evocative

Unlike other zombies, which don't care much for clothing, Day of the Dead zombies are dressed to look their best. The look is festive, usually black and white with flashes of vibrant color. Traditionally, men wear black suits and ruffled shirts, while women sport cotton party dresses in hot pink, blue, yellow, or other bright tones. Marigolds, the traditional flower of the dead, can be worn as decoration. Dusting a bit of talcum powder onto black outfits adds an otherworldly feel.

Serious Skeletons

Traditionally, people adorn their faces in skeleton makeup for the Day of the Dead festivities. You can draw the ghoulish grin of your dreams, making it as simple or as ornate as you wish. For those who really love the flesh-free look, dress in tight black outfits printed with human skeletons. You can do this yourself with black jeans, a black long-sleeve T-shirt, and fabric paint from a craft store. If you're not good at drawing, use a stencil.

Artistic Accessories

Traditional Day of the Dead outfits can be very ornate and fanciful. Think about including interesting hats, frilly or lace parasols, feathers, beaded gloves, or walking sticks adorned with a raven's head or skull. Let your imagination go wild.

Music of the Damned

While traditional Latin American zombies prefer salsa music and love songs, a new breed gathers inspiration from Mexican metal, hardcore, and goth bands such as Exsecror Vecordia, Morante, and Veneno Para Las Hadas.

Cultural Inspiration

The Day of the Dead has inspired a vast range of beautiful art. Read about the ceremonies for contacting lost spirits, and look at the amazing art created over a century ago by José Guadalupe Posada. His spooky skeletons will give you a wealth of imagery to draw on for your own attire.

TORMENT AND TERRIFY AS A NECROMANTIC ZOMBIE

Necromantic zombies are among the most horrific and deadly of all the undead legions. These demons are summoned from other realms to reside in the bodies of the dead and exist only to torment the living. Pure evil, these zombies are devoted to causing terror and insanity in all they encounter.

Pale, Rotting, and Disturbing

This zombie's look is all about the makeup. You'll want to go with a white or very light gray base for all exposed skin. Liquid-latex wounds should cover the majority of your face. Create sickly texture and slashes under your white cream-based makeup. Your mouth should be colored with the deepest of red mixed with black—although using black by itself will also work well. Use black to fill in wound slashes and create very deep circles around your eye sockets, making them look like black holes. If you can afford the investment, black contact lenses really complete the look: they'll make your eyes look like deep pits. Blood seeping out of your mouth is another nice touch.

Shred Your Outfit!

You can wear whatever you like—just make sure it's torn, tattered, and ripped. Choose clothes that you don't care about and shred them thoroughly. To rip heavier fabric, make small cuts with a pair of scissors and then rip by hand. For denim or other thick cotton, try using a cheese grater to distress the fabric. Wrap the jeans around a block of wood so that you don't cut yourself, then grate away. If you wash your clothes after shredding, more threads will unravel.

Speech Class

Here's something unusual about necromantic zombies—they can talk! Because these creatures are actually evil spirits, you'll be speaking in the voice of ancient demons. Be sure to use a lot of fancy long words to make yourself sound as if you're from a different era, and a wicked one at that! The novels of H. P. Lovecraft are a great place to find highfalutin, evil-sounding insults and antiquated expressions to fling at mere mortals.

Prop It Up

As a necromantic zombie, you were summoned from beyond the grave—yea, verily from the loathsome pits of hell (that's some of that fancy language right there). This was done with an ancient book of evil called *The Book of the Dead.* You might want to carry around an old-looking book with some mystical symbols written on the cover in fake blood. It's also not a bad idea to tote around a fake limb or head—this will make you seem especially vicious.

UPDATE YOUR LOOK WITH CLASSIC STYLES FROM THE PAST

J ust because zombies travel in packs doesn't mean they can't dress like individuals. It's never too late to update your style, and ironically, sometimes the best way to do that is to look to the past. Any period in history has zombie potential, but here are a few intriguing possibilities.

Hippie Zombie

Peace, love, and brains! What better way to flaunt your decaying flesh than with a groovy look from the freewheeling 1960s? Tie-dyed T-shirts, bell bottoms, and leather headbands are good foundations for this look. As you may have lost some (or all) of your hair, consider a visit to a wig store to find an Afro or mop top that suits you, or perhaps long, flowing, blood-drenched locks. To refine this style, focus on an iconic look from the '60s: Woodstock zombie, Andy Warhol Factory zombie, Beatlemania zombie, and so on. For humans dressing up in these zombie styles, avoid overly gruesome makeup—it doesn't fit with the era's idealistic, antiwar focus.

Flapper Girls and Dapper Gents

Whether you became a zombie in the 1920s or some other era, you can look quite smashing in this style. Female zombies should glam it up in flapper-style beaded or fringed dresses and cloche hats or headbands. Don't forget to be oh-so-daring: you're a thoroughly modern zombie party girl. Male zombies should go for a dapper suit with baggy pants and shiny two-tone shoes. Or sew your own—fabric stores carry 1920s patterns. Sleek bobs or dizzy finger curls complete the look for female zombies; males can experiment with pomade and thin mustaches. You can take this look a step further and dress as one of your favorite silent-film stars, such as Buster Keaton, Louise Brooks, Charlie Chaplin, or Clara Bow. Who knows? They may have reanimated—in fact, they could be walking among us this very minute!

Victorian Steampunk

The steampunk aesthetic combines Victorian style with modern touches—perfect for that zombie who wants to dress nicely. After all, vampires aren't the only stylish members of the undead! The Victorians were obsessed with death, so they make good zombies. In addition, their stiff, formal behavior allows you to let your rigor mortis go to work for you. Female zombies can wear corsets, bloomers, long dresses with bustles and petticoats, fancy hats, and gloves. Hair should be long and worn up in a soft bun (try pulling out some finger curls to frame your face and add a touch of romance). The gentleman zombie will look dashingly dead in a nice velvet frock coat, a pair of white gloves, and a blood-stained pair of spats. For fake-hair fun, male zombies may want to add some muttonchop whiskers and a beard.

Bog Bodies

This look is really creepy and usually reserved for prehistoric zombies who have risen from the peat-moss bogs of Ireland. Their skin is a shiny bronze color, and their limbs are contorted and surprisingly well preserved. Wear a simple, tea-stained shroud and plenty of bronzer to make this look your own. Some might think these zombies, possibly the victims of human sacrifice, are grotesques among undead culture. But they make an undeniable style statement with their stark, ancient simplicity. Be warned, however, that if you go about as a bog body, you should be prepared to argue with some who will contest that you're a mummy, not a zombie. You can tell these busybodies that although scientific debate rages on, conventional wisdom says if you're a reanimated mummy, you're a zombie. Clear on that now?

FAR-OUT LOOKS
FROM FILM AND BEYOND

Let your geek flag fly when you try out styles that take their inspiration from B movies and cult-film subculture. By now, of course, you know that not all zombies are alike. But here are some that are really, really different.

Night of the Comet Zombies

Maybe you became a zombie in 1984, after Earth passed through the tail of a comet that turned almost everyone else in your town to dust. There are two key components to your look: tons of liquid latex and fabulous '80s fashions. Comet zombies have highly

^ Scene from *Games* (1967)

textured skin and very gaunt faces (use dark makeup around your eyes and under your cheekbones to get this effect). They have big hair and dress in puffed sleeves, leggings, and rocker T's.

Shark-Fighting Zombie

Emulate one of the most popular scenes in zombie B movies with a tribute to the Italian film *Zombi 2*. While zombies in this movie are grosser and more prone to rot than many, the shark is, of course, the key. However you're dressed (the film takes place on a tropical island, so maybe Bermuda shorts?), the main thing is to carry around a shark you can fight. Try anywhere pool toys are sold.

Bride's Head Revisited

Another cool Italian zombie film is *Cemetery Man*. One zombie is a girl whose head gets detached from the rest of her body. Her parents buried her in a wedding dress, so when she appears as a zombie head, she is wearing a veil. The cemetery caretaker puts her head in a broken television set. Think about it: a zombie bride's head in a TV set! You could make the TV set out of a box and have only your head sticking out. Talk about an obscure and really cool costume.

^ Scene from *House on Haunted Hill* (1999)

Armies of the Dead

Armies of the dead are summoned to help the living in major battles, clad in the armor or uniforms they died in. This look is best as a group effort—the more friends you can get to dress up with you, the better. You can dress like Vikings, that undead army in *The Lord of the Rings*, the knights of the Round Table, World War II soldiers, Hannibal's Legion, and so on. How better to combine your love for historical reenactment and the undead in one convenient package?

Evil Corporate Zombie

Nobody likes it when a giant, heartless corporation turns its poor employees into zombies with an evil virus . . . well, nobody but the zombies, who get to have a great time eating flesh and fighting do-gooders. Dress in a lab coat with an "Umbrella Corporation" logo on it, carry vials labeled "T-Virus" filled with mysterious blue fluid, and act really, really cranky.

Japanese Rocker Zombie

In the cult film *Wild Zero*, the members of Japanese garage punk band Guitar Wolf star as themselves in a madcap adventure that involves UFOs, motorcycles, fast cars, loud music, and fire—lots of fire. The rockers battle zombies that were created by space aliens. Why not go as a zombified member of Guitar Wolf, with samurai headband, leather jacket, and smashed-up guitar?

LEND ME A HAND
FUN WITH PROSTHETICS

It's a sad fact that most zombies lose a limb at some point during their undead existence. Although it's sometimes possible to reattach a missing limb, too often circumstances—such as encounters with flamethrowers, sharks, or wood chippers—make it frankly impossible to be reunited with your appendage. But there's no reason you can't make use of the same medical innovations that humans do—in a word, prosthetics!

Where to Go

Prosthetists are experts at fitting humans with artificial limbs and extremities. Like morticians, increasing numbers of prosthetists are offering their services to the zombie population. A certified prosthetist can work with you to custom-design and fit a replacement for your missing body part.

Arm in Arm

To replace an arm, you can always go for the basic prosthetic with a grasping metal hook. Or you may choose something high-tech and realistic-looking, with fingers that can grasp objects. Depending on how open-minded your prosthetist is, you can try some custom attachments, such as a chain saw or a sword.

Get a Leg Up

Prosthetic legs come in various styles for particular uses. There are, for example, legs designed specifically for runners, hikers, and rock climbers—all good options for the zombie on the go. Don't let a missing leg keep you from enjoying your favorite sports, like chasing down your next meal!

Touching Your (New) Toes

Some zombies find that having lost toes or portions of their feet makes it difficult to walk properly. There are orthotic and prosthetic inserts to make walking easier. Inserts can fill up that space within your shoes, giving you the balance and structure you need. They may even help rid your gait of zombie lurch.

High Five!

This is a purely aesthetic consideration, but if you're missing a finger or two and don't fancy the way your hands look, there is a solution. Your prosthetist can supply you with a custom-fit finger attachment. Although it will look realistic, it won't have the same range of motion as a prosthetic leg or arm.

Tattoos

It's devastating to lose an arm or a leg, but even worse when that limb had some really rad tattoos. There is no reason you can't "tattoo" your prosthetics by way of airbrushing. If your budget is tight, maybe an artistic friend can draw something on your new limb with a permanent marker.

DÉCOR FOR THE DECAYING

Zombies are not known for their flair for decorating. But you can spruce up your domicile in ways that will prove not only attractive but also useful.

Plastic coverings work wonders. You can get the swankiest furniture you want as long as you cover it in heavy plastic.

Incense is essential—especially if you plan to have human friends over. Make sure to have several incense burners around your place to mask that rancid odor of yours.

Bars on the windows will not only keep unwanted humans out (or in, as the case may be) but will also keep other zombies from breaking into your pantry.

Hanging netting from the ceiling around favorite comfy spots will keep flies and other pests from bothering you while you're watching TV, playing video games, or reading.

Coffins make great coffee tables. Some zombies have taken to bringing their first resting place into their new residence in this useful fashion.

All doors leading from the outside world should be large, heavy, and made of metal—the better to keep humans out.

73

UNDEAD LANDSCAPING

For your own safety, it's a good idea to keep your home secure from nosy humans. But even if you're not exactly inviting garden tours, you can still include beautiful—and practical—touches in your yard. The humans needn't know what you've really got lurking in your foliage.

Disguise Barbed Wire

Barbed wire is a good way to keep zombie hunters off your lawn, but it's not very pretty. You can disguise your security fence by planting creeping plants such as honeysuckle, wisteria, or lavender. They'll obscure the fence and also create a lovely scent in your garden to mask the not-so-pleasant odors that may be emanating from your home.

Corpse Flowers

These flowers are not only beautiful but they also smell like rotting flesh. A corpse flower provides a perfectly reasonable excuse should your stench be detected and your other fragrant plantings fail to do their job of masking any unsavory smells.

Carnivorous Plants

Venus flytraps, pitcher plants, and other flesh-eating foliage are great additions to any zombie's home. You'll enjoy their carnivorous antics, but just remember—let them catch their own food (they prefer to dine on insects and other creepy-crawlies). Feeding them leftover nuggets of your victims isn't good for these delicate plants.

Utility Shed

If you have a backyard, it's smart to keep a shed with a large sturdy lock on it where you can do your culinary prep. Stock a pile of wood outside the shed and point to it if any neighbors ask about mysterious chopping noises. If your shed's got electricity, you can use it to house (and hide) a separate freezer full of your delicious leftovers.

Create a Green Screen

Tall hedges and bushes are a great way to add vegetation to your yard while maintaining your privacy. Fast-growing plants like bamboo can create a thick barrier between you and any prying eyes.

Foliage to Avoid

Smart zombies avoid planting roses or any sort of thornbush for fear of ripping their delicate flesh. Thornbushes grow really fast and can be tricky to get rid of, and you don't want to have to bring your machete every time you walk out the front door. Instead, try poison ivy or nettles. You're immune to these nasties, but they're a great way to keep humans away.

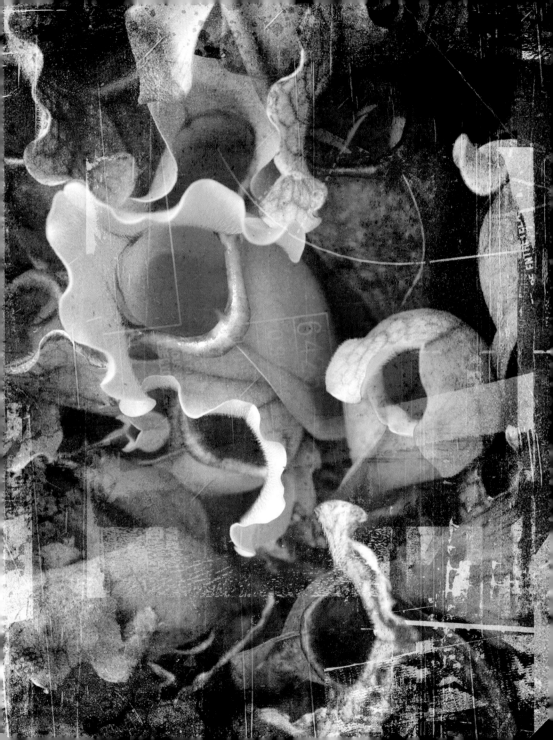

TRANSFORMING YOUR PETS

T here is major debate in the zombie community about whether it is ethical to turn your pets into zombies, but that's not to say a zombie can't enjoy the company of a furry or feathered friend—zombified or not. Here are a few facts you should consider before taking on a pet.

Monstrous Responsibility

If you're the sort of zombie who forgets to buy cat food when you're at the supermarket, then having a pet (much less a zombie pet) might not be right for you. Like you, your pet will need to feed daily, and if your pet is a zombie, it will need to feed daily on human or animal flesh. This, as you know, is harder to come by than kibble. Some zombies have a devil of a time feeding themselves, let alone making sure Fluffy has her share of fresh brains.

Method to Your Madness

Some zombies have beloved pets that they'd like to transform into their very own undead sidekicks. This tactic isn't recommended—it's best to find a cat, dog, or other friendly beastie that's already been transformed. (It's less messy, and more humane.) That being said, there are several ways of transforming your pets, the most common of which are bite or burial. Biting may produce the fastest results, but not all human zombie strains will contaminate across species. Further, you don't want to imprint on your pet's hardwiring that you caused it pain during the transformation process—you run the risk that it will decide to take its revenge on you every day for the rest of your lives! Those who have dared to make Fido a more permanent best friend have had more success with burial in a cursed pet cemetery. To find a good one, talk to your other zombie friends and ask about their results. Be aware that some pet cemeteries produce rather fearsome zombie pets, while others simply reanimate your animal friends relatively unchanged—except for their new dietary requirements, of course.

The Most Loyal Zombie Pets

Crows are known to be very intelligent and make fantastic zombie pets. Their hardwiring does not go haywire when they are transformed, and they can be very useful to their zombie owners. Cats, dogs, and rabbits make loyal pets for zombies, not to mention lovable companions. Dogs in particular are useful, as they can guard your home or keep an eye on the basement, if it happens to be stocked with live humans. It shouldn't be all hard work, though: if you happen to rip a good bone loose during a feeding spree, take it home to your dog for a game of morbid fetch.

SWEET ZOMBIE RIDE

A vintage ambulance is not only practical (lots of room for your zombie friends); it's also good for pretending you're there to help in case of a zombie outbreak. Don't forget that ambulances have handy radios, so you can call in for more paramedics if you're running low on tasty humans. (Hint: it's a good idea to have a designated human driver—your reflexes aren't what they used to be!)

ZOMBIE PARTY TONIGHT!

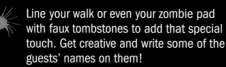

Want to have the ultimate zombie party? Here are some fun, creative ideas for the undead and living alike! Indeed, you may enjoy this home makeover so much that you never take the decorations down.

 Line your walk or even your zombie pad with faux tombstones to add that special touch. Get creative and write some of the guests' names on them!

 Buy some fake body parts from your local party or costume store and arrange them in your front garden or walkway. They'll look like they are digging themselves out of the ground to greet your guests.

Get some mosquito or camouflage netting and hang it around the house for extra creepiness. Army surplus stores are a great source for this sort of thing.

 If you have a large-screen TV, play zombie films all evening with the sound on mute. For a soundtrack, try some of your favorite zombie tunes.

 Find some old mason jars, fill them with water and a few drops of food coloring, add plastic brains or dismembered doll parts, and place them around the house.

 Buy plastic severed fingers, plastic eyeballs, and fake flies and maggots, and freeze them in ice-cube trays. This little trick will make your drinks look extra gruesome!

Replace the majority of the lightbulbs in your house with colored ones in red, blue, and purple shades to create an eerie atmosphere.

 Hang fake spiderwebs, which you can find in craft and party stores. It might look extra creepy if you put some plastic severed fingers and plastic eyeballs in the webs. Consider adding some nice big plastic spiders too.

  Nothing's more fun than a fake dead body artfully positioned in a darkened bathroom or coat closet. Freak out unsuspecting guests with a "corpse" you've purchased from a Halloween store. Or make your own with a mask, pillows or stuffing, and old clothes.

^ Scene from *Resident Evil: Extinction* (2007)

EAT OR BE EATEN

Zombies aren't known for being able to follow recipes, so here are some nice, easy party-food ideas. Let's assume you've acquired the cakes, cupcakes, and cookies at your favorite bakery or store; you've used a store-bought cake mix; or you've got access to an experienced human baker. This section is really about giving you some fun, creative ideas to make your zombie party spooktacular.

Brain Meats

A platter of various sliced meats will go over well, no matter how you present it, but do take the time to make it spooky. Choose some rare roast beef, thin slices of prosciutto, salami, and other vivid and tasty meats, and arrange them with cheese and crackers. Garnish the platter with various stuffed olives to add an eyeballtastic touch. If you want to present it in a spookier fashion, look for serving trays and bowls shaped like skulls or human heads. How better to serve meat to your human guests than from a severed head?

Blood and Guts

Cut up some fresh red fruits and make a fruit salad that looks a little bloody. Use strawberries, watermelon, and pomegranate seeds, and mix in a bit of organic (no sugar added) raspberry preserves to make it a little gooey. Sweet and succulent!

Jiggly Brains

Everyone can eat brains—even the humans— if you make some sweet, tasty brain gelatin molds! You can find these ghoulish dessert dishes at party stores and many department stores around Halloween.

Graveyard Cake

For this treat, you'll need a sheet cake in your choice of flavor, dark chocolate frosting, chocolate cookies, and lighter-colored flat oval cookies. Start by putting your chocolate cookies in a plastic or wax paper bag and crushing them with a rolling pin or meat mallet until they resemble crumbly dirt. Carefully cut the oval cookies in half, creating the shapes of tombstones. Frost your cake with the chocolate frosting, sprinkle the chocolate cookie "dirt" over the top of the frosting, and then commence designing your cemetery by placing your tombstone cookies where you see fit. Gummy worms, spiders, and other edible creepy-crawlies would also look (and taste) fantastic on this decadent dessert. For other ideas, visit a party or bakery supply store for decorations like spooky leafless trees, skeletons, and pretty much anything else your fiendish little heart desires.

Spooky Cupcakes

Use the graveyard cake method to make spooky cupcakes, placing one tombstone on each cupcake. And if you want, try writing "RIP" on the tombstones with a pastry bag or frosting tube. You can find such things in the baking section of any supermarket.

Zombie-Baby Cake and Cupcakes

Want to make your cakes or cupcakes even grosser? Use the same method as you did for the graveyard cake, but add plastic baby-doll arms in front of the tiny graves! "Bloody" the limbs with edible red decorating gel.

Zombie Cake

In New Orleans during Mardi Gras, it's traditional to serve a King Cake. This cake has a small trinket (often a small plastic baby) inside, and the person who gets the piece of cake with the baby has various privileges and obligations (like buying the cake for next year's celebration). Put a new spin on this tradition by hiding something zombie-like in your cake, such as a plastic brain. (Be sure to insert the plastic trinket after you bake the cake.) When cutting the cake, announce to your guests that there is something hidden in one of the slices. You don't want anyone to be taken by surprise—even zombies get mad when they break a tooth!

Eyeball Punch

Drain one can of lychees, then stuff the lychees with maraschino cherries. Mix 4 cups (950 ml) of lemonade with 2 cups (475 ml) of sparkling water. To create that rotting look, tint the mixture with green food coloring, then add the lychee "eyeballs." Scream-worthy!

ROCK FOR THE ROTTING

Below, you'll find a short list of zombielicious bands from all over the world. Their styles range from horrorcore hip-hop to speed metal to soulful torch songs and beyond, but they have one thing in common: Each act brilliantly evokes the gruesome world of the zombie with its original sounds and lyrics. So sit back, listen, and enjoy—you may discover a whole new world of sound for your undead afterlife.

The Cramps This American punk band was influential in founding psychobilly, which is a fusion of punk, rockabilly, surf, and deathrock. Their songs celebrate horror and B-movie clichés.

Nick Cave This Australian rock musician is known for his work in the band Nick Cave and the Bad Seeds. His post-punk/garage sound brings a bluesy feel to lyrics about the afterlife, murderers, and mystery.

Jill Tracy The beautifully evocative songs of this San Francisco–based singer and pianist are influenced in part by Alfred Hitchcock and *The Twilight Zone.*

The Tiger Lillies This brilliant and twisted British trio performs a marvelous blend of gypsy circus cabaret, English vaudeville, and Kurt Weill-esque operettas.

45 Grave This old-school L.A. band helped create the zombie-loving subgenre "deathrock." A keyboard creates an organlike effect, which—paired with the shrill female vocals—makes for a superspooky sound.

The Damned Based in London, the Damned has a melodic punk/goth sound in songs about killer clowns, space aliens, and love. Among other things.

Impaled California's preeminent goregrind band often performs dressed as zombies. And, unlike many zombies, they really like fire.

Rob Zombie No zombie band roundup would be complete without Mr. Zombie. Through his original band, White Zombie, his creepy films, and his general lifestyle, he celebrates the undead.

My Chemical Romance They swear they're not emo, just obsessed with evil and death. The song "Dead" is a heartfelt plea for love beyond the grave.

Gravediggaz One of the first horrorcore hip-hop groups, this RZA-fronted ensemble raps about horror films, cemeteries, and other fun topics for zombies.

The Misfits Danzig's original band, the Misfits helped to found the horror punk genre, and their creepy skull logo is still a classic.

Zombie Girl A Canadian electro/industrial band, Zombie Girl writes songs that feature black humor and B-movie references, while its album covers feature tasty brains.

The HorrorPops Denmark's finest psychobilly band and darlings of the Warped Tour, these gorgeous ghouls are known for clever lyrics and undead go-go dancers.

ULTIMATE ZOMBIE PLAYLISTS

Are you sad because you no longer have the higher brain function it takes to come up with an awesome zombie mix? Fret no longer, for here are some spooky playlists just for you! Think of them as your own personal soundtrack for all your voracious zombie activities.

MOOD MUSIC

The Walk — The Cure

They Are Zombies — Sufjan Stevens

Evil Dead II soundtrack — Joseph Lo Duca

Dead Souls — Nine Inch Nails

Every Day Is Halloween — Ministry

Too Sick to Pray — A3

Voodoo — Godsmack

Wave of Mutilation — The Pixies

Drawing Flies — Soundgarden

Hunting

The Dead of Night — Depeche Mode

Zombie — The Cranberries

Pet Me, Feed Me — Vermillion Lies

Bad Moon Rising — Creedence Clearwater Revival

Psycho Killer — Talking Heads

Cemetery Sal — Ragwater Revue

Thriller — Michael Jackson

PARTYING IN THE CEMETERY

ZOMBIE — FELA KUTI

PET SEMATARY — THE RAMONES

PEOPLE WHO DIED — JIM CARROLL

PRETEND WE'RE DEAD — L7

STILL OF THE NIGHT — WHITESNAKE

DEAD MAN'S PARTY — OINGO BOINGO

SIXTEENS — BODY BAG

ZOMBIE GRAVEYARD PARTY — BE YOUR OWN PET

SHE'S NOT THERE — THE ZOMBIES

6 FEET DEEP — GRAVEDIGGAZ

ZOMBIE ROAD TRIP!

Dragula — Rob Zombie

Surfin' Dead — The Cramps

Highway to Hell — AC/DC

Los Angeles Is Burning — Bad Religion

Cops Are Out — Battalion of Saints

Voodoo Child (Here Come the Drums) — Rogue Traders

The Creeps — Social Distortion

Meat House — Negative Trend

Zombie Love Songs

Smell — The Tiger Lillies

Deep in the Woods — The Birthday Party

Dead and Lovely — Tom Waits

She's Lost Control — Joy Division

Evil Night Together — Jill Tracy

The Cemetery Gates — The Smiths

Death Is Not the End — Nick Cave
and the Bad Seeds.

Haunted — Love and Rockets

A PUTRID PROM

It's not traditional for zombies to show up at school dances, but times are changing. More and more zombies are dating mortals, and you should be able to take that special someone out. You'll probably shock a few students, but you can still have an evening to remember.

Fearsome Formal Wear

Whether you decide to dress in formal wear or an outfit that expresses your individual style, a social dance is an opportunity to look your best. Gentlemen can wear anything from a tux to a zoot suit—but they should at least change from what they were wearing when they crawled out of the grave. Ladies can choose clothes in a color that suits their complexion. If you're turning greenish gray, for instance, an off-white can be nice, while for bluer skin tones, try a soft pink. Of course, basic black goes with every undead skin tone. If your arms are a bit rotten, try wearing long evening gloves. You can always enhance your best features and draw the eye away from less pretty ones. For instance, if your jaw is stuck open, be sure to emphasize those lovely eyes. If those are missing, give extra attention to your hairdo.

A Corsage for a Corpse

Gentlemen are responsible for getting their dates a corsage. Make sure to ask your date what color her dress is—you don't want the flower to clash. Of course, you can't go wrong with white, and having a strong-smelling flower like a gardenia will mask the zombie stench. Or you can get her a corpse-flower corsage and blame the smell on it!

Arrive in Style

If you're looking to make an impression, why not rent a hearse for you and your date? Call around to rental agencies to see if any specialize in unusual requests.

Meet the Parents

Some human parents may be understandably upset if their daughter's date turns out to be reanimated. Be on your best behavior and assure them you don't intend to zombify their daughter—at least not right away.

Dine Before Dancing

If you're both zombies, you can simply go out hunting together for your pre-dance dinner. Try not to get blood on your formal outfits (unless, of course, you're looking for some shock value). If your date is human, eat before picking him or her up. Then go out to a nice restaurant—and leave the waiters alone.

No Rotting on the Dance Floor

Make sure to reattach or reinforce any loose limbs with a whole lot of duct tape. You don't want anything falling off on the dance floor if you decide to flail about wildly. Slow dances are probably your best bet (and more romantic), but there's no need to take any chances. Tape up before you dress up.

GHOULISH GETAWAYS

Zombies need to take vacations just like everyone else. And if you're not lucky enough to live in a zombie-friendly city, then why not take a little trip and have yourself a fabulously horrific holiday? Remember, as a zombie you can go places no human would dare tread.

San Francisco

This city caters to zombies like no other, with zombie marches, picnics, proms, vaudeville acts, beauty contests, and more. Pretty much anytime you visit, some zombietastic event will be occurring. You should have no trouble blending right in. To explore the supernatural city, sign up for one of the walking tours that visit historic cemetery sites and crime scenes.

New Orleans

The Big Easy's historic cemeteries are known as "cities of the dead," and they're great places for the undead to hang out, too. A major cultural stop for history-minded zombies, the city boasts numerous voodoo shops, and the New Orleans Historic Voodoo Museum is a must-see. Take a spooky walking tour and, if you're lucky, you might even get to meet a real-life Voodoo Queen.

San Diego

Sunny Southern California may seem like an unlikely place to find the undead, but every summer the streets swarm with zombies attending the wonderfully geeky (and zombie-loving) Comic-Con convention. Zombies can also check out restless relatives at the haunted El Campo Santo Cemetery. If you're one of those zombies who was created by space aliens, head out to Oriflamme Mountain, where UFO sightings are common.

Rome

Italian film studios have created a vast number of fabulous horror movies, including more zombie flicks than you can shake a severed arm at. Travel to this historic city where the undead wear Armani, and soak up some culture—the locals will think you're just another film extra. Then head to the coast for some shark fighting. It's a zombie tradition!

Diyarbakir

Zombies who are really into their long-lost historical kin might visit the fabled site of ancient Babylon. It was here that the goddess Ishtar threatened to raise the first zombie army, saying that if she didn't get her way, "I will bring up the dead to eat the living. And the dead will outnumber the living." It's not too late to make this prophecy come true, just a few thousand years late. Visit this historic desert town in Turkey to launch your vision quest.

The Moon

Zombies and space have a long-standing relationship. The heck with comets; why not hitch a ride to a dead world now that you're undead? Sure, it might be hard to get a ride to orbit, but if pop stars and multimillionaires can do it, maybe you can, too. The Moon's lack of atmosphere means you won't ever rot, and the low gravity will let you bound about with ease.

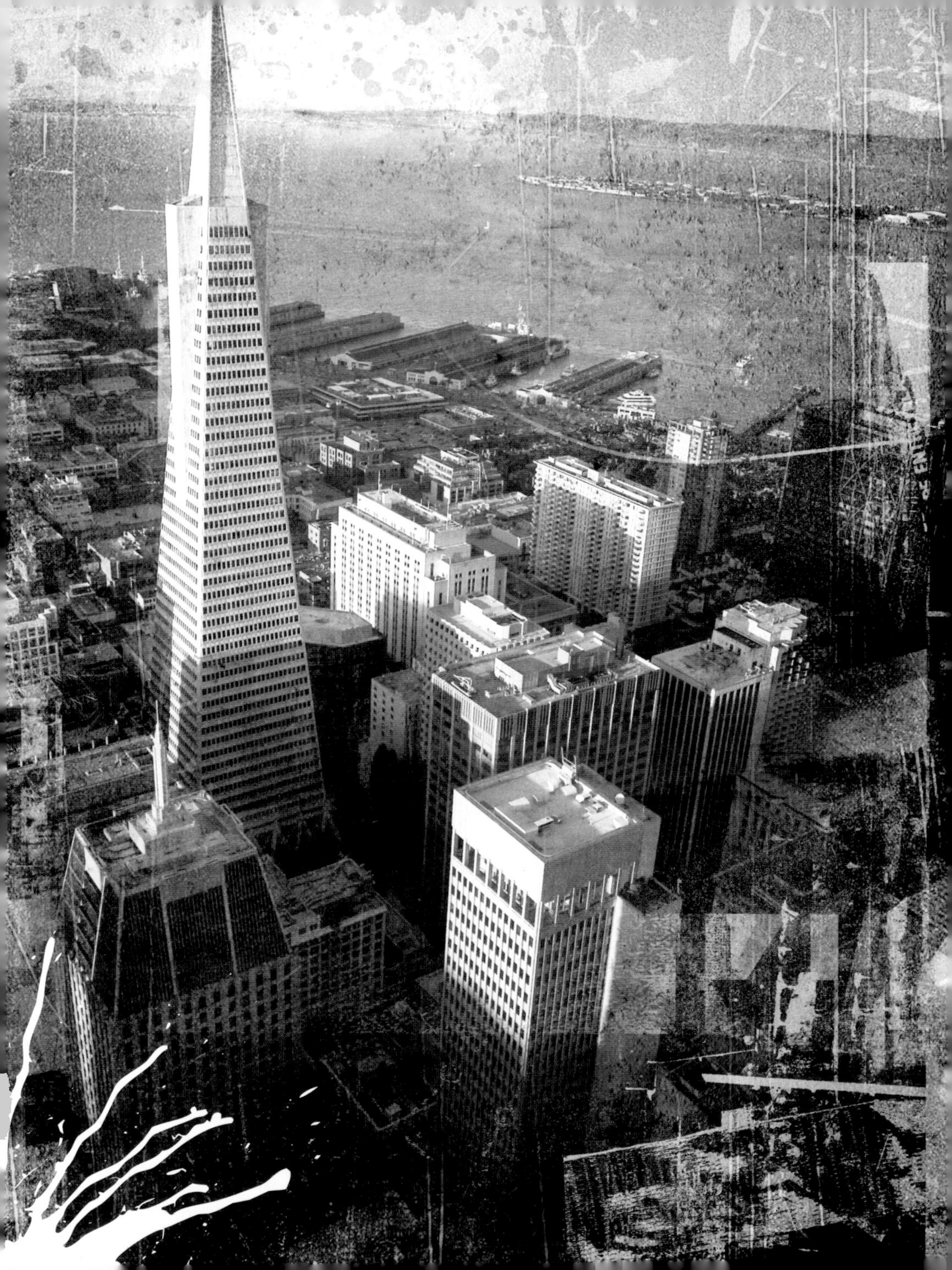

IT'S FUN TO BE A ZOMBIE!

Even though attitudes toward zombies are changing in both the living and undead communities, it's a general misconception that being a zombie isn't fun. Aside from the wounds, missing limbs, stench, and general mess, this simply isn't true. Being a zombie can be tremendously fun, and the ideas below are just the beginning. Get inspired and go have some zombie fun!

You can eat people who annoy you!

Annoying people are everywhere—only now you can do something about it! If you're a working zombie, more than likely you're stuck behind the counter somewhere, serving coffee or ringing up purchases in a local retail establishment. Humans—let alone zombies—in these positions don't ever seem to get the respect they deserve. So the next time some snooty woman barks her coffee order at you, follow her out to her car and take a big bite out of her brain. That will teach her for not tipping you!

A career in show business!

With all the zombie flicks coming out these days, who better to hire than a real-life zombie? Large film studios and indie filmmakers alike would love the opportunity to hire you for their horror films. Or have you ever fancied yourself as a carnival act? There are so many things zombies can do that humans cannot. Use your imagination and go wild!

Be the ultimate prankster!

Imagine the mayhem you can cause in the human community simply by virtue of being undead. You can create elaborate scenarios in which you are seemingly injured or killed, seriously scaring human onlookers! And if you're a zombie with a limb that's been reattached, then you know how easily you can rip off that arm or leg to frighten everyone in the vicinity!

Zombies on parade!

There is nothing more fun than running around with tons of your zombie friends, traversing your city or town, and creating a terrible ruckus! If you've amassed enough zombie friends, who on Earth is going to stop you—humans? Just eat them! If the humans are foolish enough to approach a horde of zombies, then they deserve to be eaten. So march, have fun, and show your zombie pride!

UNDEAD FUN AROUND TOWN

here are so many fun things you can do around town with your zombie friends. And there's no limit to the mayhem you can cause by sending panic into the hearts of humans while you're having the time of your undead lives!

The Shopping Mall

Yes, fiends, this one is a given—it's well known that most zombies love shopping malls. But to maximize your fun, make a plan of attack; don't just go shambling around. Pick out the swankiest, snootiest stores in your local mall, march right in, and freak those humans out. For effect, you should drop a limb or two—that will be sure to get a blood-curdling reaction out of them.

Protest for Zombie Rights

Zombies should have rights just like everyone else. They deserve health care, the right to marry humans, the right to collect their life insurance (since they are technically dead), and the right to collect disability if they lose a limb. But there are no laws currently on the books that protect zombies on important issues like job security and rights, and the government depends on your slow-witted zombie brains not to notice these things. So, get some of your human friends to help you make some signs and take your grievances to the streets with massive protests! Make your voices heard—even if all you can say is *"Braaaiiiinnnnssss."*

Cemetery Party

There is nothing more frightening for the human eye to behold than a horde of zombies rushing out of the cemetery gates. So gather yourselves en masse and take over your local cemetery. Popping up from behind gravestones can thrill both you and the lucky human you surprise. Just be sure he or she isn't holding a shovel.

Local Coffee Shop

Why can't a group of zombies meet for coffee like anyone else? Humans get so upset when they see more than a few zombies gathered in one place, but if you all just walk right in like any other customers, order your coffee politely, sit down, and enjoy your zombie selves, the humans will have no choice but to serve you with a smile. They may be a little stunned at first, and you may get more than one sidelong look from the other customers, but pay them no heed. Act as if you're doing the most normal thing in the entire world and ignore those silly humans' reactions.

Picnic in the Park

Bring your favorite edible treats and your closest zombie friends, and venture to the local park for a zombie picnic. If human friends want to join you, be sure to include treats that they can enjoy but that look gruesome enough to freak out passersby. Brain-shaped desserts, rare hamburgers, bright red punch, and other cannibalistic-looking snacks should go over well.

Freak Out the Tourists

If you live in a city that has tourist attractions, then make your way pronto with a big group of your zombie friends and give those tourists a show! Many people live their entire lives without seeing their own town's hot spots (most San Franciscans have never ridden a cable car, few Londoners tour the Tower, and so forth). Break the trend! Get your undead self out there and see the sights.

ADVENTURES IN ADVANCED ZOMBIEDOM

Congratulations, my dearly departed friends. All that remains for you now is to expand your mastery of all things zombie. In this gripping chapter, you will find thrilling and mind-altering information on essential zombie flicks that are not to be missed, eerie graphic novels featuring the undead, bloody video games, and zombies walking the pages of literature. And that's not all! You'll also find a never-before-seen zombie love story, lovingly written by me especially for you, my sweet zombie babies! So sit back and prepare yourself for the shocking conclusion of *How to Be a Zombie.*

WHAT DO YOU KNOW ABOUT ZOMBIES?

1 Name an ingredient in making a voodoo zombie.

A. Puffer fish.
B. Belladonna.
C. Nightshade.

2 You're partying and you're running low on snacks. What do you do?

A. Send out for a pizza.
B. Call dispatch and ask them to "Send more cops!"
C. End the party.

3 Name a possible origin of the word *zombie*.

A. *Jumbie*, the West Indian term for "ghost."
B. *Nzambi*, the Bantu word meaning "spirit of a dead person."
C. *Zonbi*, Louisiana Creole or Haitian Creole term for a reanimated person.

4 Name a way zombies can be destroyed.

A. Decapitation.
B. Destroying his or her heart.
C. Burning.

5 How did the rage virus first spread?

A. From infected chimpanzees.
B. From an accidental gas leak.
C. An earthquake opened a direct portal to hell.

6 What does the Umbrella Corporation make?

A. Antizombie weapons disguised as ordinary rain gear.
B. Luxury zombie-proof bunkers.
C. Bio-organic weapons—like zombifying parasites and viruses.

7 Name the book that describes a scholar's investigation of voodoo.

A. *The Serpent and the Rainbow.*
B. *The Piper at the Gates of Dawn.*
C. *Drums of Port-au-Prince.*

8 What zombifies the superheroes in Marvel Zombies?

A. Galactic rays from the Zorgon Sector.
B. The mind-control machine of the diabolical Doctor Z.
C. Bite and blood transfer.

9 Name a zombie horror comedy.

A. *Shaun of the Dead.*
B. *Fido.*
C. *Dead and Breakfast.*

10 Which band's song is featured in the film *Pet Sematary*?

A. The Cramps.
B. Alien Sex Fiend.
C. The Ramones.

ANSWERS

Award yourself one point for every correct answer, then learn your level of knowledge using the key below.

1: A

The puffer fish contains tetrodotoxin, a poison that affects humans' central nervous systems. According to voodoo lore, sorcerers use secret powders—made up of puffer-fish poison and plant-based drugs—to induce a deathlike state in their victims.

2: B

Well, of course, you would ask for more cops, silly zombie. More cops means more brains to eat.

3: All answers

Many cultures have a word for "zombie," especially in areas where zombie lore runs deep, like Haiti, West Africa, and New Orleans.

4: A & C

Even though zombies are fairly hardy sorts, decapitation will usually put a stop to their antics. Serious head wounds—like those caused by shotgun blasts—are also fatal, as are blowtorch encounters.

5: A

In the film *28 Days Later,* animal activists release infected chimpanzees from a lab. Oops.

6: C

The Umbrella Corporation is the shadowy entity responsible for an endless supply of zombie pathogens in the *Resident Evil* game and movie franchise.

7: A

Ethnobotanist Wade Davis traveled to Haiti to research voodoo practices and detailed his findings in *The Serpent and the Rainbow,* which Wes Craven later turned into a heavily fictionalized movie.

8: C

Although the Marvel Zombies series has all the comic-book goodies and intergalactic gizmos you'd expect, good old-fashioned biting does the trick here.

9: All answers

Something about zombies just seems to inspire slapstick and spoofs. If zombies weren't such fun-loving good sports about it, they might be upset that they don't get more respect.

10: C

The Ramones did a great song for this zombie-pet film, with deathless lyrics including, "I don't want to be buried in a pet cemetery, I don't want to live my life again . . . " Rad!

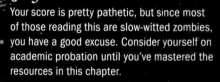

0–3

Your score is pretty pathetic, but since most of those reading this are slow-witted zombies, you have a good excuse. Consider yourself on academic probation until you've mastered the resources in this chapter.

4–7

Better, but not great. You have the desire to know more about your kind, but you just aren't there yet. Check out the suggested reading and viewing in this chapter to raise your score.

8–10

You are a zombie lord! You know everything there is to know about zombies. Seriously, you could be headmaster at Zombie College. Congratulations! You rock.

TRUE-LIFE TALES OF VOODOO ZOMBIES

While many zombies enjoy the undead life, some are forced into it. Local lore in Haiti, Louisiana, and the West Indies is the source for many zombie myths. But unlike movie zombies, voodoo zombies are living people who believe they have died and come back, becoming the docile servants of their unscrupulous master.

What Is Voodoo?

Voodoo (also known as *vodou* or *vodun*) is a religion practiced in Haiti and surrounding areas. It merges many West African beliefs with Christianity and became established in the Western Hemisphere as the result of the slave trade. In popular culture, voodoo is often synonymous with black magic and has little to do with the actual religion.

Sorcery and Potions

According to traditional belief, voodoo zombies are created by sorcerers known as *bokors*—not by bite or infection. The process involves introducing special powders into the victim's bloodstream. One traditional component of zombie powder is tetrodotoxin, a poison found in puffer fish. Some zombie experts theorize that this neurotoxin is what makes a person appear dead. Other toxins and drugs, such as datura, are added to zombie powder to induce a detached and dreamlike state that leaves the person vulnerable to suggestion and mind control. Of course, the victim's belief in the sorcerer's powers also plays a key role.

Truly the Living Dead

Victims of a *bokor* are often buried alive. The *bokor* returns later to dig up the "corpse" and force it to do his bidding (often manual labor). The person (or "zombie") is fully alive, but in a state that he or she cannot control.

True-life Terror

Many tales about people being turned into zombies by *bokors* survive. Perhaps the most famous is the real-life story of Clairvius Narcisse, a Haitian man who claimed he'd spent the years from 1962 to 1980 as a zombie. (A record of his death at a Haitian hospital provided confirmation of his story.) Narcisse inspired a host of zombie researchers to turn new attention to these living dead.

Further Evidence

Haitian laws provide tantalizing hints at the widespread belief in voodoo zombies. For instance, an 1835 law specified that anyone who administered a potion to induce extreme lethargy was guilty of attempted murder!

BOOKS TO EAT BRAINS BY

hat could be more entertaining than to read what mortal writers think—and fear—about your kind? Whether you're looking for thrills or simply want to know what antizombie plans the humans are cooking up, here is a sampling of deathless prose for the undead. Most of these books are either educational or silly, but some may be too scary for young readers. Ask your parents' permission if you're at all unsure.

The Magic Island
William Buehler Seabrook (1929)

This historical account of Seabrook's travels in Haiti was one of the first narratives to describe voodoo practices. It features black-and-white photos from the early 1900s.

The Serpent and the Rainbow
Wade Davis (1985)

Ethnobotanist Wade Davis went to Haiti in the early 1980s to investigate voodoo zombies and zombie powder. The resulting book was so influential in shaping public opinion about zombies that it received the ultimate tribute—a bad horror movie was based on it.

The Zombie Survival Guide
Max Brooks (2003)

Brooks has written the ultimate survival-manual parody for humans. Meticulously researched, this book is as frightening (for both zombies and their human friends) as it is hilarious. Read it to discover all the futile tactics humans are planning to use

to protect themselves. Armed with this knowledge, you'll be able to eat their brains!

The Stupidest Angel: A Heartwarming Tale of Christmas Terror
Christopher Moore (2004)

This novel mixes up colorful, irreverent characters, zombies, and Christmas in a California town. The supremely entertaining result is heartwarming, smartly satirical, and, of course, more than a little bit savage. What more could you want?

Zombiemania: 80 Movies to Die For
Dr. Arnold T. Blumberg and Andrew Hershberger (2006)

This thoroughly researched movie guide is a must-read for all zombies and zombie fans! Educate yourself with the classics, and discover your new favorites.

Pride and Prejudice and Zombies
Jane Austen and Seth Grahame-Smith (2009)

This book is amazing, due in large part to the deathless prose of the great Regency

Era novelist Jane Austen. However, adding zombies and ninjas to this classic romance does offer a little something extra—namely, lots of violence and tongue-in-cheek horror.

Monster Island: A Zombie Novel

David Wellington (2006)

This zombie thriller takes place in Manhattan after New York City has been completely overrun by the undead. Think you've heard it all before? *Monster Island* takes these familiar elements in unexpected and exciting new directions. Originally published online as a zombie-savvy blog.

World War Z: An Oral History of the Zombie War

Max Brooks (2006)

The product of zombie expert Brooks' seemingly boundless imagination, *World War Z* collects testimony from survivors of a zombie war. It's a fantastic commentary on government ineptitude, corporate corruption, and human shortsightedness. Soon to be a major motion picture.

ESSENTIAL ZOMBIE FILMS

Zombies—so misunderstood by humans in real life—have found enthusiastic fans on the silver screen. Filmmakers are irresistibly drawn to the possibilities zombies present. Do be aware that many of the movies considered classics are not intended for younger viewers without parental consent. Have your parents check the films out, and they will decide whether you should watch them together or not. Why not stick to the older zombie films, which are usually good, silly zombielicious fun?

Night of the Living Dead

This 1968 classic established the modern zombie movie genre. It also offers up this crucial pointer: your loved ones probably won't manage to work up the nerve to kill you, even if you do plan to repay their kindness by eating their fleshy gray matter. (However, you should look out for their less sentimental friends, who will waste no time in loading a shotgun and blowing your head off.) Also, note that neither the media nor the authorities can be counted on to accurately inform the public about a zombie epidemic. This, too, can work in your favor.

Return of the Living Dead

When there's no one left to devour, this 1985 horror comedy advises you to get on that radio and send for more cops and paramedics. We also learn that the government will gladly nuke an entire area to destroy you—so put down that snack and get out of Dodge before they blow you to bits.

Evil Dead II

This excellent necromantic primer from 1987 shows the likely results of reanimation by means of possession. One important message for everyone, undead or not, is not to mess with ancient tomes made of human flesh, or recite what's written within them. The follow-up movie, *Army of Darkness*, offers great insight into dealing with necromantic zombie kings.

28 Days Later

This 2002 British film quite literally changed how the world views zombies. With the introduction of the rage virus, zombies suddenly showed that they don't always lurch and shamble around—sometimes they can run really fast. The story of a fast-moving virus that turns humans into flesh-crazed, adrenaline-fueled eating machines, it gave a striking (and for zombies, inspiring) view of a post-apocalyptic world. It spawned the sequels *28 Weeks Later* (2007) and the forthcoming *28 Months Later*.

Shaun of the Dead

Dubbed the first romantic zombie comedy, this 2004 movie from the UK presents zombie uprisings as just another of life's little hiccups. With a steady stream of jokes and tongue-in-cheek zombie-movie references, it has inspired legions of devoted fans. Zombies watching it should note how tricky humans can impersonate zombies to dastardly effect.

^ Scene from *Shaun of the Dead* (2004)

FOR FURTHER ZOMBIE VIEWING

White Zombie

Made in 1932, this early zombie flick is about a young couple who travel to Haiti only to face disaster and heartbreak when the young woman is turned into a zombie. Bela Lugosi (of *Dracula* fame) plays a sinister witch doctor. What's great about this movie is that the humans are the villains, not the zombies.

Plan 9 from Outer Space

Often dubbed the worst film ever made, this 1959 science fiction horror film was a less-than-classic outing for the legendary Bela Lugosi. In it, extraterrestrials think it'll be a breeze to take over the Earth by raising the dead. It's one of those films that's so bad, it's actually incredibly fun to watch.

Dawn of the Dead

The message of this 1978 classic is simple: if you succumb to conformity, consumerism, and racism, you might as well be brainless, or even dead. By placing much of the action in a shopping mall, director George Romero offers up a subversive critique of late-1970s America—as well as the complete breakdown of civilization, of course.

The Beyond

This 1981 Italian fright fest directed by the awesome Lucio Fulci is filled with blood, gore, and some of the most grisly death scenes in cinema. In it, a young woman inherits a hotel in Louisiana that happens to be built over one of the "seven doors of death."

Night of the Comet

This cheesy but fun 1984 film is about a comet that passes close to Earth, causing almost everyone to turn to dust or become zombified. As they so often do, a bunch of unscrupulous scientists make matters worse.

Cemetery Man

Another awesome Italian zombie film, *Cemetery Man* (1994) features the handsome Rupert Everett as a fellow whose job is to kill the reanimated bodies that have risen from a cursed cemetery. Zombies who are missing limbs should take heart from the capabilities of the severed-head bride zombie. Missing a body doesn't slow her down as she flies through the air to attack people!

Re-Animator

This fantastically gruesome and funny 1985 movie was inspired by every necromantic zombie's favorite writer, H. P. Lovecraft! The story of a medical student who concocts a serum that reanimates the dead, it has become a cult classic with an important moral: don't try to kill your friend's girlfriend.

Braindead

Also known as *Dead Alive,* this 1992 film from New Zealand was directed by Peter Jackson (who was later widely recognized for *The Lord of the Rings* films). Funny, shocking, and disgusting, this one has it all. Use discretion if you're hanging out with humans—it's been called one of the grossest movies ever made.

^ Scene from *Zombieland* (2009)

Resident Evil

Inspired by the popular video game, this 2002 film has spawned sequels in a downright infectious manner. Another cult favorite, it offers this lesson for zombies: If the Umbrella Corporation is hiring, you might want to take that job. It's a zombie-friendly environment. Usually.

I Am Legend

Controversy arose in 2007 when this horror–action flick starring Will Smith was released. The zombies, who had taken over most of the world, were quick-moving and afraid of sunlight. While some purists decried them as too vampire-like, open-minded humans and zombies alike can take home a different lesson. Be who you are, even if haters (and buff action heroes) object.

Dead Snow

Sometimes zombies return from the dead to devastate the Earth because they're just plain evil. That's the case in 2009's *Dead Snow*, in which it's not a virus but Nazism that festers in the corpses of gruesome snowbound zombies. Strong and fast, these zombies have a weakness for stolen gold.

Zombieland

It's packed with thrilling adventure, explosions, hilarity, and of course, zombies! In this 2009 road movie, a rebel (played by Woody Harrelson) teams up with a college student with his own set of rules for surviving the zombie apocalypse. Here is a tip for zombies who may find themselves in an amusement park—avoid the gun-toting guy on the Ferris wheel. He'll blow you away!

CREEPY COMICS

Zombies and comics just seem to be made for each other. Zombies are creatures of action, favoring deeds over words. And they like bright, shiny pictures with an engaging story. The books that follow range from blackly comic to gothy and atmospheric to flat-out violent. Some may be unsuitable for the younger set, so use what little judgment you have left in the remnants of that brain of yours. Or ask a trusted older zombie for advice if you're still unsure.

Little Gloomy

This comic series was created by Landry Walker and Eric Jones. In it, Little Gloomy lives in Frightsylvania, a world where the sun never rises and the landscape is filled with monsters, such as witches, werewolves, ghosts, and—surprise—zombies. Poor Little Gloomy also suffers from the machinations of mad scientist Simon Von Simon (her ex-boyfriend), which sometimes involve Legions of the Undead.

Marvel Zombies

In this series of comics, familiar superheroes from the Marvel universe get zombified with highly entertaining (for zombies, anyway) results. Written by Robert Kirkman with art by Sean Phillips, the series features zombie versions of the Incredible Hulk, Spider-Man, Wolverine, and others trying to take over the earth as newly undead heroes and villains.

Sullengrey

This is a fantastic color comic series created by Drew Rausch and Jocelyn Gajeway. In it, the position and responsibilities of "Death" fall vacant when his son is too afraid to

accept his legacy. The result is plague, a rising death toll, and, of course, some zombie mayhem. It's a wonderful coming-of-age story, wittily written and beautifully illustrated with a dark, gothy, and stunningly detailed style.

The Walking Dead

This top-selling graphic novel series, a black-and-white monthly, is celebrated around the world, and a television series based on it is under way. Created by writer Robert Kirkman and artist Tony Moore, it features a small band of humans who survive a catastrophic zombie outbreak. While mortals find their fate quite depressing, zombies should be thrilled.

Zombies: A Record of the Year of Infection

Presented as a diary found in an abandoned cabin, this big, colorful book written by Don Roff and illustrated by Chris Lane covers one observer's day-by-day experiences of the zombie plague of 2012 (a tough year all around). It details how zombification happens and how society falls apart during the outbreak. Plus, the intriguing entries describe how the diary's author survived . . . or didn't.

^ Scene from Little Gloomy

MORE GRUESOME GRAPHIC NOVELS

28 Days Later: The Aftermath

This movie tie-in, written by Steve Niles and illustrated by a number of artists, fills in the gaps between the events of *28 Days Later* and *28 Weeks Later*. Interweaving stories show us events before the outbreak, immediately after the lab break-in that unleashes the rage virus, and new details about what happens in the days and weeks after as the virus spreads.

Blackgas

Written by comic-book legend Warren Ellis and illustrated by Max Fiumara, this dark and twisted miniseries is about what happens when an innocent couple gets trapped on an island that sits over the fault line of hell. When a tectonic shift releases an ominous black gas, the other inhabitants turn into vicious, rampaging zombies. Violence and mature themes make this one a title for the mature zombie to enjoy.

Eating Steve

Jill and Steve are deeply in love, until one night she is suddenly and mysteriously compelled to try to eat her boyfriend's brains. (Spoiler alert: Steve wants out of the relationship after that.) Deciding to move to the countryside, Jill tries to figure out what's happening to her—that is, until a zombie outbreak takes over the world, allowing her to venture out of her seclusion and join her own kind. A fantastic book by renowned comic creator J. Marc Schmidt.

Escape of the Living Dead

Taking place in the world created by George Romero's *Night of the Living Dead,* this series by John A. Russo with artwork by Dheeraj Verma picks up the story in 1971 and follows the exploits of humans trying to study and evade the zombie hordes. A motion picture adaptation is currently under way.

The Goon

A series of comics about the Goon, a muscle-bound enforcer working (apparently) for the mob. He is often bedeviled by roaming zombie hordes, as well as ghosts, aliens, and mad scientists. A recurring villain is the Zombie Priest, a gruesome character who lets no one know his name. This graphic series may disturb more delicate zombies. A movie version of the Goon's adventures is in the works.

Nightmares & Fairy Tales #1: Once Upon a Time

Written by Serena Valentino (the same writer who has guided you thus far in this volume) and illustrated by FSc, *Once Upon a Time* contains a comic that retells the story of Snow White. In this version, the wicked queen is successful in having Snow's heart ripped from her chest. But unluckily for the queen, it doesn't kill her. Rather, Snow White becomes undead—pale and ghastly, with deep black pits for eyes. And then the smart little vixen replaces her missing heart with an apple and seeks revenge on the wicked queen.

Shaun of the Dead Comic-Book Adaptation

This rendition is brought to you with the full participation of Edgar Wright and Simon Pegg, who created the classic and wonderful *Shaun of the Dead* movie. Poor Shaun doesn't have time for zombies—he's distracted by trying to sort out his troubled love life—but zombie chaos ensues nonetheless, and Shaun has to deal with it. A wonderful comic miniseries and faithful adaptation, with some fun surprises.

Zombies Calling

Written and drawn by Faith Hicks, this very funny, tongue-in-cheek story tells of three friends—Joss, Robyn, and Sonnet—who fight to stay alive during a zombie outbreak. They survive by following a set of rules they have created based on the zombie films they've seen—two years before *Zombieland*!

Zombie-Loan

Created by the manga creative team known as Peach-Pit, this series follows Michiru Kita, a schoolgirl who has the power to see when people are going to die. She is puzzled by meeting two boys who should be dead. The boys made a deal with the mysterious Zombie-Loan office to stay alive, but have to hunt zombies in return.

BEREN COUNTY
SHERIFF'S OFFICE
11 27 38
42799

▽ Artwork by Karl Christian

JULES AND VIOLET

True love never dies . . . that's what the poets tell us. But what if someone you love becomes a member of the undead? It's one of those difficult relationship issues so many couples are facing these days with zombification on the rise. Here is a touching, twisted tale of how two people in love handled this problem. Read on if you dare, and meet our mismatched sweethearts in this special-edition, exclusive zombie comic.

BEST ZOMBIE BOARD GAMES

Zombie board games? Really? It's true; the world of zombie gaming is not limited to your computer or game console. For those zombies who find themselves without the necessary technology, or for those who just like to kick it old-school, some fearsome fun awaits. Although board games date back as far as the ancient Egyptians, these games are more recent. Try one for a zombie family night at home.

Last Night on Earth

Brought to you by the fine folks at Flying Frog Productions, this game forces small-town heroes to rally against a multitude of zombies. Players can choose to act as heroes or zombies in a number of interesting scenarios that allow cooperative play. It's good strategic practice to get your zombie skills down before an attack! Plus, the game comes with a CD soundtrack of original music, and many delicious expansions await.

Oh No . . . Zombies!

Prepare to find yourself smack in the middle of a zombie outbreak! This Archie McPhee game places humans across a cursed cemetery from the storeroom housing shotguns, radios, and other essentials that might help them survive—if they can get there without being eaten. Practicing human survival brings valuable knowledge about how to anticipate human actions and how to hunt them. Ever heard the phrase "Know your enemy"?

Zombies!!!

This Twilight Creations game is different every time you play it, thanks to a board made of movable tiles. The object is simple: get to the helipad. To do that, though, you must evade zombies and unhelpful friends—and be thrilled by a plethora of extras, like glow-in-the-dark zombies, zombie dogs, and many expansions. Take advantage of the fact that humans are usually too focused on deceiving one another to notice you sneaking up on them.

Zombiegeddon

Another winner from Twilight Creations, Zombiegeddon is a quick-paced strategy game. Begin by rushing around town and gathering supplies, then spend the rest of the time trying to survive. The winner is whoever has the most valuable stuff when play is over. The moral? Humans are selfish and greedy and only concerned with their own survival. Bonus: cyberzombies will be happy to know that there is an electronic version of this game.

ZOMBTASTIC VIDEO GAMES

ombies star in many great computer games. Be warned, many of the most famous games require parental consent to buy or play. Ask your parents to look at game reviews and decide whether they feel comfortable with your playing these games. Luckily, there's a wealth of all-ages games available to the young zombie, so everyone can play.

Plants vs. Zombies

Try this silly but surprisingly addictive game available on multiple platforms (iPhone, Microsoft Windows, Mac OS X, Xbox Live Arcade, and Nintendo DS). In it, you must fill your garden with zombie-fighting plants in the hopes of staving off the flesh-eating undead. Highlights include "zombie bowling" and a surprise celebrity zombie appearance.

Alive-4-Ever

Formulated for the iPhone and iPod Touch, this fast-paced mobile game offers an RPG-like experience system and four basic zombie-fighting characters to choose from. The game has 30 levels and makes good use of the touch-sensitive screen. Great to play while shambling about town.

The Last Guy

A PlayStation 3 puzzle game that takes you and the few zombie apocalypse survivors through a variety of international sites while you fight the undead. Cool street-level maps make the locations superealistic, and your zombie foes get increasingly dangerous.

Tales of Monkey Island

The latest installment in LucasArts' popular voodoo-themed game suit, this episode is available for both the Wii and Windows. The exciting thing about this game for zombies is that, rather than killing your undead buddies, you get to play as the zombie pirate Guybrush Threepwood and search for various voodoo artifacts.

Teenage Zombies

This Nintendo DS game actually manages to make brain-eating seem endearing. Perhaps its wide popularity will help humans realize that zombies can be cute and cuddly.

Other Games

Any search for zombie-related games will turn up lots of games rated for mature players. Your parents will be the best judges of whether these games are okay for you to play, so be careful when you see reviews of top-rated games including Call of Duty 5, Dead Space, Halo 3, Left 4 Dead, Resident Evil, or others not reviewed above, and ask your parents if they are okay for you to try.

Scene from *Resident Evil: Extinction* (2007) >

Humans obsession with zombie culture has spawned many books and films, all dedicated to studying our undead ways. Why so curious, you ask? Perhaps these mortals are attempting to exorcise their nightmarish fantasies about the fragility of life. Or maybe they're just jealous of all the havoc-wreaking fun.

v Scene from *Grindhouse* (2007)

GO FORTH AND DEVOUR

These are my final words to you, my zombie darlings, so take heed. Now that you are armed with an arsenal of undead knowledge, use it well and venture out into the world. Nothing can stand in your way when you're comfortable in your own (rotting) skin, aware of how you've been transformed, able to socialize with zombies and humans alike, well versed in zombie lore and culture, and—last but not least—stylishly dressed. Share this tome with others of your kind so they, too, may join your fearsome horde better informed, properly equipped, and ready for the inevitable zombie apocalypse. At the very least, you and your friends will be ready for a rousing zombie march through your city's streets. So go forth, my zombie sweets, to bring disorder, panic, and squeamishness to your human foes while inspiring your human friends to join in the zombie mayhem. I hope to see you at a march!

ENRICH YOUR BRAINS

GLOSSARY

Apocalypse

The catastrophic damage to or utter obliteration of a civilization. A zombie apocalypse comes about as a result of a zombie outbreak.

Army of the Dead

A group of undead warriors summoned from beyond the grave by magic to help turn the tide of a battle.

Bog Bodies

Mummified remains found in the bogs of northern Europe. Scientists believe they may have been buried in unhallowed ground as punishment for crimes in life, making them prime zombie candidates.

Bokor

A voodoo sorcerer whose magic is said to have the ability to create zombies.

The Book of the Dead

A sinister tome featured in the *Evil Dead* movies. Not to be confused with the ancient Egyptian funerary text of the same name, this fictional book was inspired by the *Necronomicon* in stories written by H. P. Lovecraft, and contains information on summoning evil spirits.

Comet

A midsize body orbiting the sun (bigger than a meteor, smaller than a moon). If a radioactive comet crashes on Earth, it can zombify those in the area.

Corpse Flower

Found in the Sumatran rainforests, this enormous flower is said to smell of rotting meat.

Day of the Dead

A Mexican holiday (el Día de los Muertos) on which the dead return to celebrate with the living.

Expansions

Extras for board games that include new scenarios to play, making your gaming sessions even more thrilling.

Half Dog

Dogs that have been sliced in half for medical teaching purposes. They're encountered in zombie form in *Return of the Living Dead*.

Hardwired

Refers to an innate trait that requires no thought or learning and is difficult if not impossible to change.

H. P. Lovecraft

An American horror, science fiction, and fantasy author who lived from 1890 to 1937. Lovecraft is most commonly known for having created the Cthulhu mythos, among other frightening tales.

Incantation

A recitation of specific words for summoning spirits or performing magic.

Kuru

A disease believed to be caused by eating human brain tissue, found primarily among cultures with a history of cannibalism.

Liquid Latex

A rubbery liquid that dries after application. It is often used in special-effects makeup for many purposes, including creating realistic-looking wounds.

Maggots

Fly larvae, usually residing in decaying flesh.

Morgue

A place where dead bodies are kept until they can be identified and claimed for burial.

Mortician

An undertaker or other professional who prepares the dead for funerals and burials while assisting the families during their time of grief.

Necromancy

The practice of communicating with or summoning the dead. Necromantic zombies are spirits summoned into dead human bodies.

Neurotoxin

A poison that affects the brain, causing brain damage, paralysis, death, and zombification.

Outbreak

The sudden or aggressive beginning of something unsolicited such as war, disease, or . . . zombification!

Prosthetics

Artificial limbs such as arms and legs for those who may have been born without them or who lost them due to injury. A prosthetist is a specialist in this field.

Rage Virus

A zombifying virus causing extreme violence in those infected. Zombies created by this virus are distinct from others in that they move extremely quickly; they were first documented in the movie *28 Days Later*.

Reanimation

The restoration of dead to "life" through sorcery, science, cursed cemetery, or some other means.

Rigor Mortis

The stiffening of the joints and muscles of a body a few hours after death. This phenomenon is responsible for the jerky, stiff, and awkward bodily movements that most zombies exhibit.

Steampunk

A style of dress that merges elements of Victorian garb with cyberpunk fashions.

Tetrodotoxin

A powerful neurotoxin that is a poisonous compound present in the ovaries of certain puffer fishes. It is a common ingredient in zombie powder.

Trioxin

A fictional nerve agent from the *Return of the Living Dead* films. Its release from faulty canisters caused humans in the vicinity to become zombified.

Voodoo

A religion practiced in the Caribbean and the southern U.S. that merges elements of Roman Catholicism and African rituals, and distinguished by ancestor worship, sorcery, and spirit possession.

Zombie Powder

A secret mix of powdered substances used in voodoo rites to put a person into a deathlike state.

Zombie Virus

A virus causing zombification in those infected by exchanging bodily fluids (such as blood or saliva), by the consumption of tissue, or as the result of those tissues becoming airborne through incineration, spewing of fluids, or other means.

Zombie Walk

An annual gathering of humans who like to dress as zombies and walk through the city streets in their full undead glory.

RESOURCES

Even certified, card-carrying members of the undead must answer to some authority from time to time. Make sure to clear all zombie activities and reading material with your parents.

Zombie Walks

Auckland (New Zealand). The Annual Auckland Zombie Walk happens in October and features prizes for costumes, plus an Armageddon Expo!

Frankfurt (Germany). The annual Zombie Walk takes place in July and encourages all zombies in every style to partake in the fun.

Rio de Janeiro (Brazil). The annual Crawl of the Dead journeys from Copacabana to Pedra da Gávea, where they enjoy a beautiful view and tasty brains. Held in November.

San Diego (United States). The San Diego International Comic-Con Zombie Walk is held annually during the convention in summer. All are welcome to drag their bloody corpses through the Gaslamp District.

San Francisco (United States). The SF Zombie Mob is held every year. This two-hour zombie walk through the city streets causes much havoc, with a fun after-party to follow!

Sydney (Australia). The Sydney Zombie Lurch and Halloween Party takes place on Halloween, and features a march followed by horror films and a fancy-dress party.

Toronto (Canada). The Toronto Zombie Walk gathers some 1,000 members of the undead to march, celebrate, and watch scary movies. Takes place in late October.

Further Reading

Deadworld, by Stuart Kerr and Ralph Griffith (1987–2009). This ongoing comic-book series, and soon-to-be major motion picture, tells the story of the world some months after the zombie takeover.

Highschool of the Dead (2006–2008). This Japanese manga series follows a group of high-school students as they battle growing legions of zombies.

The Living Dead (2008). This anthology of zombie stories includes writers from Stephen King to Neil Gaiman.

Breathers: A Zombie's Lament, by S. G. Browne (2009). A newly reanimated zombie has trouble adjusting.

The Forest of Hands and Teeth, by Carrie Ryan (2009). A teen struggles with the religious rules of a village comprised of survivors of a zombie apocalypse.

INDEX

Copyright © 2010 by Weldon Owen Inc.

All rights reserved. No part of this book may be reproduced, transmitted, or stored in an information retrieval system in any form or by any means, graphic, electronic, or mechanical, including photocopying, taping, and recording, without prior written permission from the publisher.

First edition 2010

Library of Congress Cataloging-in-Publication Data
Valentino, Serena.
  How to be a zombie : the essential guide for anyone who craves brains / Serena Valentino.
    p. cm.
  Includes index.
  ISBN 978-0-7636-4934-0
  1. Zombies. I. Title.
  GR581.V35 2010
  398'.45—dc22 2010003253

16 15 14 13 12 11 10
TTP
10 9 8 7 6 5 4 3 2 1

Printed in Huizhou, Guangdong, China

A Weldon Owen Production
415 Jackson Street
San Francisco, California 94111

Candlewick Press
99 Dover Street
Somerville, Massachusetts 02144
visit us at www.candlewick.com

WELDON OWEN INC.
CEO, President Terry Newell
Senior VP, International Sales Stuart Laurence
VP, Sales and New Business Development Amy Kaneko
VP, Publisher Roger Shaw

Executive Editor Mariah Bear
Editor Lucie Parker
Project Editor Heather Mackey
Editorial Assistant Emelie Griffin

Associate Creative Director Kelly Booth
Designer and Illustrator Scott Erwert
Assistant Designer Meghan Hildebrand

Production Director Chris Hemesath
Production Manager Michelle Duggan
Color Manager Teri Bell

Special thanks to Jacqueline Aaron, Michael Alexander Eros, Marianna Monaco, and Gail Nelson-Bonebrake.

Photography

All images courtesy of Shutterstock, with the following exceptions:
Scott Erwert: 48 **iStock:** 10–11, 38, 58, 61, 63, 70, 75, 77, 89, 100, 132
Picture Desk: 22–23 (*28 Days Later,* 2002 / DNA/Figment / Fox / The Kobal Collection / Peter Mountain), 41 (*Undead,* 2003 / Spiergfilm / The Kobal Collection), 42 (*Blood of the Zombie (The Dead One),* 1961 / Mardis Gras Productions / The Kobal Collection), 47 (*Fido,* 2006 / Lions Gate / The Kobal Collection), 56 (*Dawn of the Dead,* 1978 / United Film / The Kobal Collection), 68 (*Games,* 1967 / Universal / The Kobal Collection), 69 (*House on Haunted Hill,* 1999 / Warner Bros. / The Kobal Collection / Peter Iovino), 81 (*Resident Evil: Extinction,* 2007 / Constantin Film/Davis-Films / The Kobal Collection), 105 (*Shaun of the Dead,* 2004 / Big Talk/WT 2 / The Kobal Collection), 107 (*Zombieland,* 2009 / Pariah Films / The Kobal Collection), 123 (*Resident Evil: Extinction,* 2007 / Constantin Film/ Davis-Films / The Kobal Collection), 124–125 (*Grindhouse,* 2007 / Dimension Films/A Band Apart / The Kobal Collection) **Kira Siegfried:** 2–3, 6, 13, 94, 96–97 **Serena Valentino:** 5 **SLG:** 109

All image treatment and photo collaging by Scott Erwert

All illustrations by Scott Erwert with the following exceptions:
Juan Calle (Liberum Donum): *Zombie Love* 112–119 **Karl Christian:** 111

Front cover illustration by Scott Erwert based on a photograph by Konstantynov

3567405288582○

CHASE BRANCH LIBRARY
17731 W. SEVEN MILE RD.
DETROIT, MI 48235